DIANA
WARRIOR PRINCESS

Witty Words By
Marcus L. Rowland

Amazing Art By
Aaron Williams

Lazy Layout By Matthew Goodman

Words Copyright 2003 By Marcus Rowland
All Illustrations Copyright 2003 By Aaron Willams
This Presentation Copyright 2003 By Heliograph, Inc.
Lucky ISBN: 1-930658-13-3.

Body Text is ITC Benguiat By Ed Benguiat
Titles and Ornaments are Greymantle By Kanna Aoki

HELIOGRAPH INCORPORATED
www.heliograph.com
26 Porter Street • Somerville, MA 02143 USA

CONTENTS

Introduction

Diana paused at the edge of the ravine and listened. Nothing but the howl of a distant coyote, the soft slither of sand blown by the wind, and a faint hiss of steam from the crashed helicopter's boiler below. But she could sense there was something out there. She silently pulled herself over the rocky edge, checked her sword and bow, and crouched, waiting.

Fergie slid up beside her, cupped her hand to her ear, pointed, and whispered "That way..."

Diana turned slightly and listened again. Now she could hear it; faint music, drums and the soft twang of a sitar. "Indians..."

Diana: Warrior Princess is a modern-day role playing game with a difference.

Imagine our world, as seen by someone as remote from us as we are from the ancient Greeks, and with as many gaps in their knowledge. Then imagine it converted into a TV series by a production company showing the loving attention to historical accuracy we have come to expect from such series.

Throw realism out of the window. Run adventures in which Eva Peron is Hitler's mistress, or JFK meets Queen Victoria. Zulu hordes swarm across Vietnam, the Spanish Inquisition stalk heretics in Manhattan, steam cars co-exist with ICBMs, Babbage engines, stealth bombers and sorcerers.

Later sections describe the game rules and give full details of the major characters of the series. First comes the game's setting, the world of *Diana: Warrior Princess*. It should be made clear that while the game world is modelled on a TV series, and the rules emphasise the cinematic nature of the campaign, it's the real world as far as the characters are concerned. It's just a real world that behaves very oddly by normal standards...

If this doesn't appeal an appendix describes some alternate campaigns in which this is a virtual world, used for entertainment purposes or as a punishment for its unwitting inmates.

Acknowledgements

This setting is based on ideas originally discussed on the soc.history.what-if and rec.arts.sf.fandom newsgroups, and on the CIX what-if and rpg.uk conferences. Many thanks to all those who contributed to the discussions, and especially those who encouraged me to develop the setting into a complete game. Characters were suggested by Ashley Pollard, Mike Cule, John Dallman, and Megan Robertson. Tim Illingworth provided operatic information. Many thanks to playtesters at Rocococon and Gencon 2001 for their suggestions.

Important source of inspiration for this game were the books *Motel of the Mysteries* by David MaCaulay, an inspired parody of archaeology, *How Britain Won The Space Race* by Desmond Leslie and Patrick Moore, an "alternate history" of space travel, and two "articles" on the future archaeology of London, *The Discovery of London* by G. H. Boden (1903) and *When The New Zealander Comes* by "Prof. Blyde Muddersnook, P.O.Z.A.S." (1911).

The main mechanisms of the rules were suggested by the combat system used in the war-games *Aeronef* by Matthew Hartley and Stephen Blease and *Full Thrust* by Jon Tufley, all of whom have kindly allowed me to adapt them to this game. Participants in the CIX rpg.uk and sjgames.roleplaying conferences and members of Rocococon helped immensely with comments and play-testing. In particular Vicky Cox, Diana Cox, Paula Dempsey, Steve Dempsey, Lynne Hardy, Madeleine Eid, Ian Miller, J.V. Meekins, Paul King, and two others whose names I've lost were invaluable in debugging the rules. Thanks to Darrin Bright, Kevin Mitchum, Paul King and Alex Stewart for plot and character ideas, and to Steve Jackson for his guest appearance.

An earlier and somewhat different version of the setting appeared in *Valkyrie Magazine* issue 23, August 2001, under the title "Diana: Amazon Princess."

The World

Diana's world is our own,
seen dimly and through a distorting mirror,
adding gods, magic, and Mystic Powers.

Adventures usually begin in England, which is rural (apart from London, a sprawling walled metropolis) and ruled by the autocratic Queen Elizabeth; she dislikes Diana (who divorced her son) and wants her dead. The Queen is aided by Thatcher the Sorceress, who secretly plots to overthrow Elizabeth and impose an even more tyrannical rule. The nearby country of Britannia is ruled by Queen Victoria, whose red-coated Beefeater armies are feared by all. Scotland is a land of mists and kilted bare-chested barbarians, who generally appear driving spike-festooned steam cars, a loose association of clans ruled by Queen Mary. Ireland has mists, sorcery, and leprechauns.

Europe consists of vaguely-defined countries (such as France, Germany, and Huy Brazil) mostly overrun by Nazis, Queen Victoria's Beefeaters, and the armies of other war-lords. Africa is jungle, the Middle East camels and pyramids, America is also divided into several nations and combines high-tech with steam locomotives, cowboys and river steamers.

Treat the geography, politics, and economics of this world as fuzzily as possible; mountains and other natural features seem to move to meet the needs of the plot, and there should be ample room for an extra country or two if needed. Maps should be avoided if possible, and if not should be obviously wrong (an upside-down map of Australia labelled as "Africa", for example). Money exists, but is rarely seen except as a bag of gold, a copper or two paid for a drink, a reward, or the object of a robbery. Characters always seem to have enough for their immediate needs, without a huge surplus.

Transport ranges from sailing ships and carriages to steamboats and trains to airships (with sails) to supersonic fighters and space shuttles. Whatever most advances the plot is available, and any vaguely plausible technology is used regardless of anachronism, with extra knobs, dials, and switches added to 20th century "black box" gadgets.

For example, a cellphone is a book-sized box with two long extending aerials sparking in a "Jacob's Ladder" effect. Calls are made via a human operator and text messages come out of the side on ticker tape, but it is nevertheless possible to call to and from anywhere in the world. CDs are played on phonographs with horns and lasers for "needles". Steam cars may get their heat from peat or nuclear reactors.

A cellphone is a book-sized box with two long extending aerials sparking in a "Jacob's Ladder" effect. Calls are made via a human operator and text messages come out of the side on ticker tape, but it is nevertheless possible to call to and from anywhere in the world.

The Cast

There are two main characters, others turning up on an irregular basis, plus hordes of extras. Players can take on these roles or develop their own; several alternate series with this general setting are described below. Characters should be

Diana dedicates her life to Peace, fighting war (and the war-god Landmines) whenever she encounters it (or him).

based on (or at least named after) well-known figures of 19th to 21st century history, but greater anachronisms can creep in. Find full statistics for the more important characters in handy photocopiable format on page 57.

Diana was an "ordinary" Princess until she began to suspect that her husband, Bonnie Prince Charlie, was unfaithful. While seeking evidence she discovered his involvement in a hideous black-market trade in arms and the deadly drug "tobacco", both sold to children in third-world countries, and responsibility for the deaths of thousands of innocents.

Diana immediately denounced and divorced him. Somehow she retained the Mystic Powers of Royalty after the divorce, despite being Royal by marriage, not birth, while Prince Charlie lost them. She has since dedicated her life to Peace, fighting war (and the war-god Landmines) whenever she encounters it. Somehow this dedication gives her superhuman strength and speed. This behaviour has earned her the enmity of Queen Elizabeth, who wishes to silence her permanently. She has since escaped from kidnapping and assassination attempts, but must be wary whenever she is in England. Landmines also wants to stop her, but hopes that he might be able to "turn" her to his side.

Diana always wears spotless leathers which function as armour; she and her clothing stay clean even if she has been wading through mud or blood, it's one of the Mystic Powers of Royalty[1]. Others include healing (of obscure diseases such as the King's Evil, Scapie, and Lepus[2], phenomenally accurate aim with her bow and arrows, and the ability to jump tremendous distances. She can operate any vehicle including motorcycles and cars, steam trains, tanks, boats, mecha, airships and other aircraft, space shuttles, and lunar landers. She can also ride horses, camels, and other animals. She should be by far the most skilled warrior and martial artist in the campaign. She will always try to use her weapons to stop an opponent, not to kill.

A typical quote: "I'll bring peace to this land if it kills us all..."

---

1. "How do you know he's a King?"
"He isn't covered in shit."—*Monty Python and the Holy Grail*
2. King's Evil = Scrofula, Scapie = mad sheep disease,
Lepus = rabbits (a small mistake by the scriptwriters).

FERGIE

Fergie is remarkably unlucky and is the most likely candidate to be bitten by a vampire, venomous snake or radioactive spider, kidnapped, hypnotised, enchanted, or abducted by aliens.

Fergie is Diana's sidekick, a country girl of good (but vaguely defined) background who has somehow attached herself to the Warrior Princess. She is superficially a dumb redhead, has a heart of gold, and is very good with children and animals. Appearances can be deceptive; she is smarter than she looks, a competent martial artist and an expert hunter and tracker, and carries a sword and at least two concealed knives at all times. She kills if she feels it is necessary, and seems to do so fairly often; while she respects Diana's goals, she occasionally disposes of enemies that Diana would leave alive, if she thinks she can do so without Diana finding out.

Fergie is remarkably unlucky and is the most likely candidate to be bitten by a vampire, venomous snake or radioactive spider, kidnapped, hypnotised, enchanted, or abducted by aliens.

Quote: "I don't know, one of his enemies must have caught up with him..."

RED KEN

Red Ken is a barbarian hero who aims to free London from the rule of the sorceress Thatcher, who rules the city and bleeds its citizens of their wealth and freedom.

WILD BILL GATES

Often seen running from angry mobs, Wild Bill Gates is a skilled gambler, quick-draw gunfighter, and occasionally competent computer programmer (using punched cards and tape), famous for his slogan "Make Money Fast".

Red Ken is a barbarian hero who aims to free London from the rule of the sorceress Thatcher, who rules the city and bleeds its citizens of their wealth and freedom. Thatcher's most deadly assassin, the enigmatic Archer, is on his trail but has so far failed to kill him. Red Ken is a skilled martial artist and knife-thrower, but his main expertise is with animals; he can ride superbly, and his pet lizards, salamanders, frogs and snakes seem to obey his very thoughts and have saved Diana or Fergie's life on several occasions. Diana doesn't entirely approve of Ken, since he believes that Thatcher's crimes justify the use of lethal force, but there are ambiguous hints that they have at some stage been lovers. There are also hints that he and Fergie have been lovers, or that all three have shared some sort of relationship. He seems to be more of a member of the "team" than Diana's other allies.

Quote: (looks at a frog making "gurkk" noises) "My little friends tell me that there is a stranger in these woods..."

Wild Bill Gates is a river-boat gambler and entrepreneur who tends to turn up with dubious schemes whenever the action moves to America, and occasionally takes them overseas. He is often seen running from angry mobs. He is a skilled gambler, quick-draw gunfighter, and occasionally competent computer programmer (using punched cards and tape, of course), famous for his slogan "Make Money Fast". He is a loyal ally of Diana, with suggestions he would like to be a good deal more, and will reluctantly risk his life to save her. A useful role model is Brett Maverick. There is intense friendly rivalry between Gates and Red Ken. There is unfriendly rivalry between Gates and Hubble (below). Both despise Prince Charlie.

Quote: "I didn't say the land I sold you was above water..."

Ron L. Hubble is a more blatant con-man; he and Gates hate each other, and both try to out-do the other's scams. Most of his rackets, such as a "miracle radiation cure" based on molasses, involve an element of pseudo-science. He is most notorious for selling NASA a space telescope designed so badly that it had to be fitted with spectacles. He is much less lucky than Gates, and is on the run from several warlord's assassins. Diana saved his life once and lived to regret it. Fergie plans to kill him if possible, although she doesn't give it a particularly high priority.

Quote: "OK, so the diet pills contained tapeworm eggs. People lost weight, didn't they?"

RON L. HUBBLE

Ron L. Hubble is a blatant con-man
most notorious for selling NASA a space
telescope designed so badly that it had to be
fitted with spectacles.

Bonnie Prince Charlie is Diana's ex-husband. He isn't a bad person but is easily led and extremely suggestible, frequently mind-controlled by his mother, who can see through his eyes and take over his body at will; this is signalled by his eyes changing colour, by a change in speech and stance, and by the use of horrific casual violence. He collapses afterwards. Diana and Fergie are not aware of this evil; somehow it always happens when neither is in a position to observe him, and they (and he) always assume that someone must have knocked him out.

He can fly jets and helicopters, ride a horse, and shoots reasonably well. He should be played as comic relief when in

Bonnie Prince Charlie is Diana's ex-husband.
When in his own mind, he turns up to pester
Diana with flowers and other gifts in an attempt
to persuade her to remarry him at the most
awkward possible moment.

He isn't a bad person but is frequently mind-controlled by his mother, who can see through his eyes and take over his body at will; this is signalled by his eyes changing colour, by a change in speech and stance, and by the use of horrific casual violence.

his own mind, turning up to pester Diana with flowers and other gifts in an attempt to persuade her to remarry him at the most awkward possible moment. Often these gifts are prompted by his mother and contain traps for Diana; for example, a jewelled pendant might be cursed, stolen from someone extremely powerful, or contain a bug or a small bomb. He tries to help Diana, but his clumsiness and his mother's influence usually means that it all ends in tears.

Quote: "I say, Diana, couldn't we... you know... get together again?"

Landmines, God of War is a half-man, half-machine hybrid, brutally attractive, who incorporates numerous weapons into his body. His right hand is made of metal; a regular series joke consists of him saying "let me give you a hand", or variants thereof, giving it to a victim who is grabbed then engulfed in flames as it explodes. He makes frequent attempts to "turn" Diana, usually by tricking her into killing an innocent. He then plans to make her his mistress, and transform her into the unstoppable magical cyborg of his dreams. Landmines can be killed, but since he is a god he always returns. He usually appears as the dark power behind a warlord or some act of oppression.

Quote: "You have failed me, but I am moved and even slightly amused by your grovelling. Here, take my hand..."

Other Gods rarely play a major part; Landmines has staked his claim on Diana and the other gods usually respect it. Others include FedX the messenger of the gods, his sister AmX the god of wealth, Tesla the god of lightning and storms, and Buro, master of the celestial civil service. Old Nick O'Teen is the demon lord of disease and pollution. Gods and goddesses of Love, Fate, Mischief, Death, etc. may also appear.

Queen Elizabeth rules England; she is secretly the criminal genius known as the Queenmother, involved in international arms and tobacco trading. She wears a crown, long white gloves, and an ermine robe covering armour. She is extraordinarily strong with strange mind control powers (possibly a property of the crown), used mainly to "manage" her son and husband (who is rarely seen and appears to be in the last stages of senility), and to punish underlings who fail her. Her mace can project a stream of energy, apparently magical in origin, which can inflict pain, burn, or age its victims while simultaneously rejuvenating the Queen. Fortunately it is deflected by mirrors, and one always

LANDMINES, GOD OF WAR

A half-man, half-machine hybrid, brutally attractive, who incorporates numerous weapons into his body. A regular series joke has him saying "let me give you a hand" as his metallic right hand turns into an exploding grenade.

seems to be around when the ray is used. Her ungloved touch can cause disease. It is apparent that she has been seduced by the Dark Side of the Mystic Powers of Royalty. Her palace is full of death traps, escape chutes, hidden panels, and concealed weapons. She has returned from apparent death on several occasions, usually finding Charlie or Thatcher attempting to rule England in her place. She is an ally of Landmines, but plans to depose him and take his place as God of War. She or her underlings are likely to appear in any adventure set in England.

Quote: "Now my plot has Diana in its coils, and soon she will pay the price of her disobedience. Nyah-ha-ha-ha-ha!"

Queen Elizabeth rules England; she is secretly the criminal genius known as the Queenmother, involved in international arms and tobacco trading.

THATCHER THE SORCERESS

Thatcher the Sorceress is Queen Elizabeth's chancellor and adviser. In London most public areas have a gigantic poster of Thatcher... the eyes occasionally glow red and follow the movements of passers-by. She employs hordes of tax collectors in a variety of guises; 'Traffic Wardens', 'Inland Revenue', and the dreaded 'Poll Tax Collectors' and 'VAT Inspectors'.

Thatcher the Sorceress is Queen Elizabeth's chancellor and adviser, but appears to be plotting to seize her throne. Thatcher has several duties, the most important is squeezing taxes from London, which she does with ruthless efficiency. Her powers let her disguise herself and underlings as other people or inanimate objects, suppress light in any enclosed space (such as a room), telekinesis, and levitation. Most Londoners believe that she is undead, and since she is never seen outdoors by day and has no reflection it is possible that they are right. In London most public areas have a gigantic poster of Thatcher, usually guarded by uniformed thugs. The eyes occasionally glow red and follow the movements of passers-by. If Thatcher makes an announcement (usually of a new tax) the posters animate. Sometimes graffiti artists try to deface the posters; they typically suffer unlikely accidents (think of *The Omen*) within moments. There are also statues of Thatcher at various points around the city which are rumoured to be giant golems, although no-one has ever seen them move. The largest is on top of the column in Trafalgar Square. She is supernaturally beautiful, probably a magical illusion. She employs hordes of tax collectors in a variety of guises; 'Traffic Wardens', 'Inland Revenue', and the dreaded 'Poll Tax Collectors' and 'VAT Inspectors'. Like Queen Elizabeth, she has apparently been killed but returned on several occasions. She often appears if an episode is set in London.

Quote: "You can't pay? There really is no alternative. Guards, take him away..."

Thatcher has a good twin, the mysterious Mother Theresa. A master of various martial arts, she sometimes appears in flashback in Diana's thoughts. She is said to be as powerful a magician as Thatcher, although her magic is used for good. It seems likely that one of Thatcher's schemes will eventually involve taking her place, or using her as bait in a trap for Diana.

Archer the Assassin is Thatcher's ultimate weapon. He(?) is never seen, except as a cloaked and hooded figure with gloved hands, and there are hints that he may be the evil twin of one of the major series characters; probably Red Ken or Fergie, possibly Diana herself. It isn't certain that Archer is male or even human. His weapons include crossbows with poisoned bolts, rifles, throwing knives and stars, sword sticks, lasers, and poisons. He seems to be seriously unlucky, since his attempts to assassinate Red Ken and Diana have consistently failed, or may be playing a deeper game and missing intentionally. He only appears as Thatcher's accomplice, never on his own.

Quote: (in a hoarse whisper) "The Lady Thatcher sends her greetingssss..."

Archer the Assassin is Thatcher's ultimate weapon. He(?) is never seen, except as a cloaked and hooded figure with gloved hands, and there are hints that he may be the evil twin of one of the major series characters

PRINCE ALBERT EINSTEIN & QUEEN VICTORIA

Queen Victoria rules Britannia (England's neighbour), a rapidly expanding empire spread by her fierce red-coated beefeater soldiers.

Queen Victoria rules Britannia, England's neighbouring kingdom, whose capital is the city of Windsor[3]. She is the benevolent monarch of a rapidly expanding empire spread by her fierce red-coated beefeater soldiers[4]. She argues that the countries they conquer are happier under her rule, which may be true, but doesn't convince states bordering her empire. Britannia has many claims to fame, not least The Bomb developed by Victoria's husband, Prince Albert Einstein. Victoria has mixed feelings about Diana; she likes her and appreciates

3. Windsor, Ontario, with a large castle added.
4. Warriors joining her armies swear to eat nothing but beef, to absorb the mystical power and energy of the mighty ox.

Beefeaters & John Brown

Victoria's escort is a few beefeaters and
her fierce woad-daubed Scots bodyguard
John Brown, a legendary barbarian warrior
typically armed with throwing axes, a bandoleer
of grenades, a two-handed sword and an AK-47.

her good intentions, but isn't prepared to let her jeopardise the security of Britannia or the expansion of the Empire. Sometimes Diana thwarts her plans; within days Victoria, a military genius, comes up with new strategies. Diana and Fergie are welcome at her palace, since Diana has twice helped to save Victoria from Elizabeth's assassins. Naturally various map rooms and command bunkers are kept firmly locked when they are around.

Victoria does not believe in Landmines, but several of her Generals are dedicated to his service. If Diana can show her he exists Victoria may turn to the cause of peace.

Victoria has her own Mystic Powers of Royalty, including a force screen which has saved her from several assassination attempts and a healing touch. Her powers also enforce the oath sworn by beefeaters, who will never betray her; when Elizabeth infiltrated agents into Victoria's bodyguard they switched allegiance on taking the oath, and are now fanatically loyal servants of Victoria. She is never armed, but always escorted by a few beefeaters and her fierce woad-daubed Scots bodyguard John Brown, a legendary barbarian warrior typically armed with throwing axes, a bandoleer of grenades, a two-handed sword and an AK-47. Stories set in Britannia are likely to involve her or her Empire.

Quote: "You wish our armies to withdraw? We are not amused..."

Prince Albert Einstein is Victoria's consort, a German prince and scientist who spends most of his time in a laboratory. His inventions include The Bomb (never described more clearly), land leviathans, flying dreadnoughts, cruise missiles, and other weapons to make warfare "too horrible to contemplate". Most of the world's warlords happily contemplate such horror, and several now use his inventions, so he has begun trying to persuade Victoria to set an example by endorsing Diana's cause. He won't help Diana disrupt Victoria's plans, but won't do anything to stop her. He also has Mystic Powers of Royalty, mostly manifested as invulnerability to laboratory accidents and other minor disasters.

There have been attempts to kidnap Albert and steal the plans of The Bomb. Oddly Queen Elizabeth doesn't appear to be after it, implying that she may have it or something worse. Albert is likely to appear in any story involving Victoria, if only in the background.

Quote: "Ach so... Oh well, back to the drawing board..."

Emperor Norton is benign ruler of large parts of America. He has the Mystic Powers of Royalty, mainly luck and persuasiveness verging on hypnotism, and amazingly fast sleight of hand. He can produce anything from a rabbit to a bazooka from his top hat, and often does so. He always seems to be able to produce small items such as a gun or lockpicks from nowhere, even if he has been repeatedly searched.

He is a fat jolly bearded man who wears a top hat and frock coat and smokes a corncob pipe. He is interested in space

EMPEROR NORTON

Emperor Norton is benign ruler of large parts of America. He can produce anything from a rabbit to a bazooka from his top hat.

travel and is the founder of NASA (Norton's Agency for Space Achievement), which is preparing for the first expedition to the Moon.

Norton is secretly an alchemist, and in laboratories under his palace at Fort Knox has rediscovered the Philosopher's Stone, as well as building a golem, which is used to stir the cauldron in which the gold is made. Norton intends to use the gold to buy weapons and turn them into more gold, until there are no more weapons in the world. Diana is aware of these plans and can see some flaws; she isn't convinced that giving money to weapons manufacturers is a good idea. Nevertheless his heart is in the right place, and he secretly helps to fund her campaign against war. Norton is guarded by the Secret Service (all of whose agents wear jackets with the Secret Service logo, an eye in a pyramid).

Quote: "You will observe that there is nothing up my sleeve..."

Norton's state is a constitutional monarchy, with the day to day affairs of the state handled by an elected parliament currently run by President Kenny. See the adventure "Diana Does Dallas" for more on Kenny.

Other parts of America are ruled by "Uncle" Sam, a paranoid "Big Brother" style demagogue whose state practices universal conscription and is continually at war against largely imaginary enemies, and King Martin Luther, notable as a religious reformer. There are also Indian[5] territories, vast wildernesses, and anything else that seems appropriate.

Milosovitch, Stalin, Napoleon, Churchill and Mao are typical world leaders, warlords in the service of Landmines. They all lack the Mystic Powers of Royalty, since they have obtained their thrones by conquest, fraud or assassination. Usually they have several competent generals and vast numbers of warriors who are basically cannon fodder. For example, Stalin has generals North and Rommel and Mongol hordes, mostly riding coal-fired steam motorbikes. Typical Quote: "Kill them, you idiots!"

In addition to the above, there are dozens of petty warlords and bandits who at any time may descend on a peaceful village, hold up a train or hijack an airship. Other dangers include groups of wandering religious fanatics (from Thuggee to the Spanish Inquisition), hostile savages (such as Indians in America, Zulu tribesmen in Vietnam, and so forth), and wild animals ranging from coypu to sabre-toothed tigers, mostly completely inappropriate for the location where they are found.

5. Apparently Sikhs.

A Typical Episode

Titles

Montage of WW2 tanks, Cruise missiles, Zulu warriors, etc. Dramatic music.

Narrator: "It is a time of great evil, when the hordes of the war-god Landmines stalk the Earth..."

Cut to Diana (who wears a small crown) driving an open-topped car into a parking garage, stomping into the Queen's office in Buckingham Palace, banging her fist on the table until tea cups rattle, throwing a ring on the Queen's desk and the crown on the floor, and stomping out.

Cut to Queen (wearing a larger and somehow more sinister crown), coldly furious, tearing a picture of her son (also wearing a small crown) and Diana apart.

Narrator: "Humanity called for a champion..."

Cut to Diana (now in a small apartment) throwing clothes into a suitcase.

Cut to a sinister horse-drawn hearse outside, and two Men In Black carrying a yellow gas cylinder to the door.

Cut to fumes coming through the keyhole. Diana lights them with a convenient candle.

Cut to cylinder exploding outside and the building catching fire.

Narrator: "She was Diana, Warrior Princess...."

Cut to Diana (who is suddenly clad in tight white leathers and carrying a complex longbow) walking out of the blazing building, getting a motorcycle from a stable next door, and riding off to fight evil.

Narrator: "A warrior to oppose war."

Diana And The Grapes Of Wrath

Diana and Fergie are walking through the woods around London when Fergie is bitten by a rabid wallaby. Diana cauterises the wound then puts Fergie into a mystical trance, in the care of a nomadic coypu-herder, while she heads off in search of Louis Pasteur, the one man who can heal her; this involves running along roads dodging or vaulting over steam cars for a while, then entering a quaint 20th-century city labelled "Paris" (and looking like Moscow). She interrogates some gendarmes (who

Pasteur is playing a trombone to a large tub of grape vines (the first historical pictures of anyone named Louis the researchers found were Louis Armstrong and Joe Louis).

wear Gestapo uniforms) to find the clinic, where Pasteur (who is black; the first historical pictures of anyone named Louis the researchers found were Louis Armstrong and Joe Louis) is playing a trombone to a large tub of grape vines, trying to see if music will cure the fungus which is threatening the grapes of France. He won't talk to Diana until she has proven she is a worthy warrior, by taking him on in the boxing ring; naturally Diana wins.

Diana wants Pasteur to help Fergie, but he explains that if the grape disease isn't stopped nothing will save France's wine. And if France can't send Queen Victoria her annual tribute of wine her beefeaters will invade through the Channel Tunnel.

Meanwhile in London the coypu now have rabies, shown

RABID COYPU

The coypu have rabies,
shown as red eyes and fangs.

as red eyes and fangs; the nomadic herder's mobile home is surrounded, and they are leaping up against the windows to try to smash their way in.

Back in Paris Diana suggests that her Mystic Powers of Royalty can cure certain diseases; maybe this is one of them (she hasn't tried it on Fergie's rabies; this is never explained). She concentrates, and there's a little flicker of lightning as the mould drops off and the grapes are restored to perfect health. "But there are millions of grape vines in France" says Pasteur.

Easy, says Diana, the healed grapes will in turn cure them if the person handling them is an innocent; cut to scene of dozens of children dancing through the vineyards in white tunics and necklaces of flowers, touching the grapes and transferring Diana's Mystic Power to them. Pasteur gives Diana the rabies cure, a large decanter of green medicine which must be drunk in a single swallow.

Meanwhile Landmines, a handsome cyborg god, is angered at the failure of the disease, and sends a few Hells Angels to fight Diana before all the grapes are cured; if she kills anyone before the last grape is healed they will all sicken again (for no readily apparent reason)...

Meanwhile the rabid coypu seem to have disappeared, and the herder cautiously climbs out to get some water. As he stands by the mobile home there's a sudden growling noise (which we have come to associate with rabid coypu) and he is dragged under, screaming, and leaving the door not quite locked...

Cut to Diana trashing bikers...

Cut to coypu trying to pry the door open...

Cut to Diana running back along road...

Cut to door popping open...

Cut to Fergie lying on the bed, still unconscious, as coypu close in...

Cut to Diana running through woods again...

Cut to coypu opening its mouth to bite...

Cut to arrow flying through air...

Cut to coypu going "eep" and falling over...

Cut to Diana firing arrows at superhuman speed...

Cut to Fergie stirring fitfully and starting to froth at the mouth...

Cut to Diana walking through field of skewered coypu...

Cut to Fergie (who now has red eyes) opening her mouth (which now has fangs) and turning towards Diana...

Cut to Diana using martial arts to immobilise Fergie without hurting her, then shoving the decanter into her mouth and making her drink...

Cut to Fergie's eyes gradually returning to her normal colour...

Cut to Diana letting Fergie up...

Cut to Fergie and Diana walking through the woods and Fergie saying that she could really go for a jug of French wine...

Disclaimer: No rabid coypu were harmed in the making of this episode; however, large quantities of grapes were accidentally squashed.

Creating Episodes

The main theme of a campaign should be Diana's attempts to bring peace to a war-torn world. Often she must choose the lesser of two or more evils; for example, saving part of Victoria's empire from conquest by Stalin's Mongol hordes. Secondary themes include Elizabeth's attempts to eliminate Diana, Ken's attempts to depose Thatcher, and other long-term problems. Diana should usually be the focus of adventures, but it is entirely possible to run adventures without her.

There are several tricks, common to historical research and to the excuse for it that is often seen on TV, that can be used to produce new settings and characters, to surprise and entertain players:

Telescoping is the trick of collapsing time when looking at the distant past; for example, by making Queens Elizabeth and Victoria contemporaries.

Transcription Errors are the tendency for details to get confused as they are copied, especially where records are poor. A common error is to replace a name with something else that sounds more familiar; Eva for Evel, Nell for Neil, and so forth.

Conflation is the tendency of myth-makers and historians to confuse historical figures, events, and organisations which have similar names or backgrounds. For example, Prince Albert Einstein is a conflation of Prince Albert and Albert Einstein. The version of Louis Pasteur described in the program outline is a conflation of Louis Pasteur, Louis Armstrong, and Joe Louis. Use this trick a lot, it always gets a laugh.

Mythologising (or "a plausible hypothesis...") is the bad historian's way to avoid saying "I don't know". See, for example, the explanation for the name of Queen Victoria's Beefeaters.

Plots should emphasise action, adventure, and humour; logic is of secondary importance, implausible coincidences and last-minute plot switches are everyday occurrences. Think of a typical action-oriented TV series, with a plot twist or a fight somewhere in every segment. The script example above shows how a typical episode runs, although Fergie gets less action than usual; Diana's main aim is to save Fergie, but she also saves France from Victoria's beefeaters, upsets Landmines' plans, and gets to trash some thugs and rabid coypus along the way.

Adventures should ideally be run with no more than two or

three player characters; larger groups tend to get in the way of the action, or find that the Star and one or two others are doing 90% of the work. If it is essential to use a larger group it is probably advisable to find a way to split them into two or more separate teams, working together or at cross purposes. Ideally keep the Star and Co-Star as one group, Guest Stars as the other, and organise encounters appropriately. Alternatively, think about setting up a more team-orientated campaign based on a larger group with common goals; there are some examples of alternate campaigns below.

Keep the action fast, simple, and generally funny, but occasionally give the characters a mystery to solve or a complicated obstacle to overcome, or confront them with a tragedy. Always keep things moving; if the players seem to be bogging down, throw in a fight scene, some scantily clad dancers, or whatever else seems likely to get them moving again.

Episode Treatments

Plan Nine From Outer Mongolia

Spurred on by Landmines, Stalin hatches a new plan; his Mongol hordes will invade Japan. Japan is a series of islands, so the biking horde might encounter problems—but Landmines tells him that Prince Albert has developed a freezing ray used to prepare the mountains near Windsor[6] for the next Winter Olympics. In Stalin's hands it will be used to freeze a road across the sea. Stalin contacts Elizabeth and arranges a trade; if her spies will capture the ray machine for him, he will give her a six month lease on his hordes once Japan has been captured. Diana and Fergie must chase the machine across Europe and Russia, dodging assassins, to an eventual confrontation with Stalin and his generals at the head of the invading horde. In playtesting this ended with Diana and Fergie adrift on an iceberg, all that was left of the invasion route, which was promptly rammed by the *Titanic*...

---

6. There are no mountains near the real Windsor. There are no mountains near Liverpool, but that didn't stop Donizetti from setting an opera in them in the 19th century.

It's Only A Game

A new craze sweeps London; a hand-held computer game in which players must fit falling geometric shapes to make increasingly-complex patterns. They are on sale everywhere, ridiculously cheap, and everyone seems to be playing. But the game is addictive, with a hypnotic effect on its players. It drains their free will and initiative, and reduces their resistance to Thatcher's tax collectors and Elizabeth's mind control. Diana, Fergie, and Ken trace them back to their source, a factory apparently owned by their old friend, Wild Bill Gates! Is the American entrepreneur aware of their real nature, or has he been tricked into making them? Is there any cure for the addiction (which now has Fergie in its grip)? And is there any way to turn their sinister power back on Elizabeth and Thatcher, or on Landmines himself?

Diana's Birthday

Diana lets slip that it will be her birthday in a few days. Fergie and Ken both want to find her the perfect present. Charlie mentions that one of the gems from Elizabeth's mace would be the ideal gift, "but of course mummy would never part with it." Will they work together to steal the gem, or at cross purposes? Will they be able to make it a surprise present? And why has Charlie made the suggestion; could the gem be a lure for the capture of Diana's friends, or cursed in some way?

Romancing The Scone

(Based on an idea by Alex Stewart)

Red Ken learns that Charlie has bought a haggis[7] farm in Scotland. He asks Diana and Fergie to help check it out; Charlie has a history of unethical investment, and Ken is worried that the haggis may be kept inhumanely, or that the farm may be a cover for something more sinister.

When they reach the farm they soon realise that Ken's suspicions are right; there are a dozen guards, surprisingly

---

7. Small animals valued as a delicacy, with an unfortunate habit of escaping and getting underfoot at suitably comic moments. They look like little furry balls with legs.

tough fighters who will fight to the death, mostly clustered around a building that looks like a prison. Inside they will eventually find a group of druids led by the charismatic arch-druid Rabbi Burns. Once rescued Burns explains that he and his druids were waylaid while transporting the legendary Stone of Scone to Balmoral for solstice celebrations in three days. Without the Stone the celebration can't take place, Queen Mary's Mystic Powers will be lost, and the Scottish throne will fall. An invasion by Elizabeth's hordes will probably follow. But the druids have only been prisoners for a few hours, and there is nowhere nearby an aircraft might land. It's likely that the Stone is being transported overland and is still in Scotland. Diana or Fergie can track it. Naturally the Druids (all reasonably skilled martial artists armed with deadly bagpipes[8]) tag along.

In fact the thieves work for Victoria, not Elizabeth; her agents have purchased the farm in Charlie's name, and will blame Elizabeth if anything goes wrong. Her Beefeaters are poised to invade after the solstice. Meanwhile the mercenaries are transporting the Stone by pack-mule through the mountains (don't ask...) towards Britannia. It's in a wooden casket shaped like a house-boat, and is roughly the size of a brick. It seems to throb with Mystic Power, but only the rightful ruler of Scotland can use it. If anyone else opens the chest bad things will allegedly happen—how bad is left to the referee.

Meanwhile Elizabeth has also learned of the theft of the Stone, and plans to have her own goons intercept it. Once it is in her power she will force Mary to marry Prince Charlie and England will absorb Scotland. All three forces converge in the mountains. If you want to get really silly Charlie also turns up, with a small group of incompetent mercenaries; the only woman he wants to marry is Diana, so he's anxious to see the Stone restored to its rightful owner. Needless to say they will mostly get in the way.

With luck the fight ends with the Stone of Scone in Diana's hands, and restored to Mary for the coronation. The episode ends with Rabbi Burns ceremonially placing the Stone under a leg of Mary's throne (which was broken centuries ago), so that she can sit down for the solstice ceremonies without the throne collapsing. Fade out to a happy ending, and a nice haggis dinner...

---

8. Lung-powered acoustic weapons. Only druids know how to use them.

The Gnus Of Marylebone

In a surprise move Thatcher announces the closure of London Zoo; all its animals will be slaughtered in a week. Red Ken is heart-broken, and wants to organise their rescue before the deadline. He and his supporters in the London underground plan to evacuate them to safe-houses around the city; as part of his scheme a herd of gnus must be moved from the zoo to a warehouse in Marylebone, where they will be loaded onto a sailing barge for shipment out of town. When the gnu-herder is trampled by a stampeding herd of zebra, a replacement is needed in a hurry. Of course Fergie has always been good with animals, but the panicking gnus will soon stretch her patience to the limit, and make her think that no gnus is good gnus... As the evacuation continues, the jaws of Thatcher's trap begin to close—the animals have been fitted with tiny transmitters, and her "tax-collector" thugs can track them to find Ken's supporters. But of course Diana and Ken will be expecting trouble...

Rocket To The Moon
(based on an idea by Paul King)

Following a mysterious explosion Diana's friend Nell Armstrong, a NASA (Norton's Agency for Space Achievement) astronaut, is trapped on the Moon. Nobody else has a craft ready to rescue her ... except, perhaps, for weird scientist George Stephenson, who is currently experimenting with a rail-launched rocket. His spaceship might be able to reach the moon, but lacks the fuel to make a round trip. However, it happens that Prince Albert Einstein has been working on the problem of propulsion. His fuel is much more powerful than Stephenson's and would allow the round trip but may literally make the spaceship "go like a bomb", and as usual the lackeys of various foreign powers seem to be interested in stealing its secrets. As the seconds tick by and Armstrong's air supplies run low Diana and her friends must convoy the fuel safely from Windsor and across the border into England, then to Stephenson's launching site in the wilderness near London, fighting off bandits and Thatcher's evil Poll Tax Collectors. Then there's another problem; the pilot, Eva Kneivel, has been shot in the last fight and is in no condition to fly the mission. Who will volunteer to take her place? And if they do eventually rescue Nell, what was the real cause of the explosion?

Gnome on the Range

For centuries the Gnomes of Zurich, a race of grotesque cave-dwelling dwarves, have been on good terms with humanity. They love intricate toys such as cuckoo clocks, and while they have no gift for mechanics they are excellent miners and buy their trinkets with gold. Suddenly they are refusing all offers of trade, and anyone entering their caves is tarred, feathered, and thrown out without explanation. The economy of Zurich is declining, and the city fathers call on Diana (who just happens to be in the area) for help. Fortunately even gnomes respect the Mystic Powers of Royalty, and eventually explain that they are fed up with their mountain being used as the backstop for the Swiss Navy's firing range.

It turns out that the Navy has just bought new and much more powerful guns for their mighty warships, and are indeed testing them on a gunnery range a few miles out to sea from Zurich. Unfortunately the guns, while amazingly powerful, are less accurate than their predecessors, and accidents will sometimes happen... Diana must persuade the Swiss Navy to abandon the tests before the gnomes are actually killed—at the moment they just have bad headaches—and find out who was responsible for the introduction of the new guns before someone really gets hurt or the Swiss economy collapses.

Disclaimer: No real princes, princesses, monarchs, former prime ministers, mayors of London, best-selling authors, or billionaires, living or deceased, were injured in this study of the evolution of history into myth. However, certain TV series which show even less regard for historical accuracy got what was coming to them...

More Series

While this game concentrates on Diana: Warrior Princess, it isn't the only series with this setting. There are several others, sharing a common background and some of the villains and supporting cast. Usually there is little or no overlap of the main characters, although a guest appearance by Diana or one of her allies is always fun. Characters from these series might also turn up in a Diana-centred campaign. Here are a few examples:

Elvis—The Legendary Tours

In this action and music packed series fighting troubadour Elvis searches for the key to the lost Land of Grace, a mystical kingdom which has been trapped behind a magical barrier. Armed only with his guitar, his revolver, and seven-league blue suede boots he wanders the world fighting evil and searching for clues to release his ancestral home. Aided (and often hindered!) by bickering musician companions Vlad Lennon and Joe "Senator" McCartney, his adventures really rock!

Parton—Lust For Glory

A hard-hitting gritty military series in which tough General "Dolly" Parton, Amazon mercenary, leads her band of women warriors and their cyborg camels through the desert hell of the Korean war. Parental guidance is strongly advised, since most episodes feature scenes of graphic violence. Supported by an expanding range of Cyber-Camel Corps toys and games.

Toni The Vampire Slayer

London, a city tormented by the evil of the undead sorceress Thatcher. Her sinister powers are slowly destroying the barriers which protect humanity from the supernatural. While the London Underground fights Thatcher's human henchmen and servants, her undead allies are less easily suppressed. Fortunately there are warriors to oppose them; by day their leader poses as meek schoolgirl Toni Blair, by night she fights the hideous forces of darkness as Toni the Vampire Slayer.

Gandhi's Angels

On the mysterious island of Manhattan the ancient monk Mahatma Gandhi trains three women warriors in the fighting arts, and uses his powers to send them into the world on a series of mystical quests. The exciting adventurers of "Babe" Ruth, Marion Morrison, and Toni Curtis involve magic, martial arts, horror and suspense, and the story arc leads to a crescendo of terror as the secrets of the sinister "Ivy League" are slowly unearthed.

Richard of Hollywood

After dictator "Uncle" Sam seizes power deposed duke Richard Nixon decides to fight the usurper in the forests of Hollywood. Soon his outlaws become feared as they rob from the rich to feed the poor and confront the Dark Forces responsible for Sam's rise to power. Join Richard, Tiny Tim, Will Shakespeare, Maid Marilyn, and the rest of the outlaw band in these exciting stories.

The (Brief) Rules

This is not a realistic system; it sets out to be as cinematic and melodramatic as possible, and as easy to play as possible given that intention. It is thus wide open to rules lawyers and power gaming—if you want a system that doesn't reward such abuse you should probably look elsewhere. The author assumes familiarity with the ideas of role playing games, since he doesn't want to write yet another "this is how an RPG works" section that will go unread by 99% of his intended audience. You will need several six-sided dice per player—twenty or more may be needed to run powerful characters such as Diana or Landmines, God of War. In all that follows the author is fully aware that the singular of "dice" is "die"; he just doesn't care.

Characters have sixteen attributes, with a minimum value of 0 and maximum of 10. The total number of points available for attributes is the character's Status, their importance in the series, which is explained below.

Status is initially determined by the referee, but may be improved in play. For example, a Star has status 40 (and may gain more status with experience), so initially spends 40 points on attributes. Status also determines the success number for the character and the number of hit points, found by dividing status by 5 (round up). Some examples of characters and status are shown in the table.

Status/Success	0-19/6	20-49/5+	50+/4+

ROLE	STATUS	SUCCESS	HITS	EXAMPLE
Star	40+	5+	8	Diana
Co-star	30+	5+	6	Fergie
Guest Star	20-30	5+	4-6	Red Ken, Victoria
Speaking Extra	15	6	3	John Brown
Extras	10	6	2	Secret Service agents, thugs
Cannon Fodder	5	6	1	Most soldiers
Peasant	2	6	1	Paul the Peasant
Sergeant	10	6	2	Beefeaters
Henchman	20-30	5+	4-5	Archer the Assassin
Villain	30-40	5+	6-8	Thatcher
Major Villain	50	4+	10	Elizabeth
Minor God	20-40	5+	4-8	AmX, Goddess of Wealth
Major God	50+	4+	10	Landmines, God of War

Players should usually run characters with at least 20 Status; Stars, Co-Stars, and Guest Stars. Several suitable characters are listed below, but players may prefer to design their own. If so they should be based on personalities from the "real" world who would be likely to be remembered many years in the future; famous politicians and rulers, scientists, and other celebrities. There need be little or no resemblance between the character and the real person; in fact, it's often more fun for there to be a complete contrast. Characters from mythology or fiction could also be used, if it seems plausible for them to enter the historical record, but again there should be distortions.

Attributes

Attributes are used by rolling one dice for each point in the Attribute.

Animal Handler: Riding and other feats of animal control.
Artist: Painting, singing, gourmet cooking, etc.
Athlete: Leaping, climbing, etc.
Charisma: Star quality and/or ability as a leader.
Computers: Programming and using them.
Driving: Control any vehicle including aircraft.
Healing: Medical and first aid skills, and laying on hands.
Luck: What it sounds like.
Marksmanship: Combat with guns, bows, throwing weapons, and other ranged weapons.
Martial Arts: All hand-to-hand and hand-held weapon combat.
Mystic Power: Uncanny abilities (defined by the Referee). Characters only have Mystic Power if the Referee allows it.
Science: Knowledge of nature and the universe.
Speed: Ability to react quickly, dodge, and move fast. Also determines who attacks first in combat.
Strength: Any feat of strength other than combat.
Thief: Picking locks, pockets, sneaking around, forgery, etc.
Thinking: Solving puzzles, general knowledge, flashes of inspiration.

Example: *Red Ken has Animal Handling (6) so will usually roll 6D6 for this attribute.*

Any roll greater than or equal to the character's success number counts as one success; all dice that roll a success are rolled again. Repeat until no more successes are rolled, or until it is obvious that more successes would be wasted effort. The total number of successes shows the degree of success (explained below).

Example: *Red Ken wants to ride a wild stallion. He uses his Animal Handling skill rolling 3, 2, 5, 6, 4, 5; his success number is 5 so he has rolled three successes. These are re-rolled as 3, 3, 5, one more success, which in turn is re-rolled as a 4. In all he has rolled four successes.*

Sometimes the roll is made without reference to the activities of other characters or NPCs; for example, using a Computer roll to find the password for a network, using Thief to pick a lock, using Healing to cure someone's injuries, using Martial Arts to hit someone who isn't expecting it as above. At other times characters may be opposed by other characters or NPCs, and victory will be determined by the total number of successes rolled on either side.

Optionally unusually easy tasks can be accomplished without rolling dice, even if there are no points in the relevant attribute; for example, almost anyone can drive a car on a deserted road by day, even if they have little or no training. Things get more difficult at night, or when there is rain or more traffic. There are three important exceptions; nobody gets to fight without points in Martial Arts or Marksmanship, or uses Mystic Powers without at least one point in this attribute!

Most ordinary things can be done by rolling a single success. More are unnecessary, but represent unusual grace or skill.

Difficult things may need two successes; for example, most armour absorbs at least one hit, so two or more successes are needed to harm someone wearing it.

Sometimes difficult actions require the use of two or more Attributes, such as Martial Arts and Strength (to throw someone across a room), or Driving and Marksmanship (to fly a plane and operate its guns). To do this simply add the attributes, and roll the appropriate number of dice.

Example: *Wild Bill Gates has Luck (3), Thinking (3), and Thief (3). In a difficult poker game he might use Luck plus Thinking (6 dice) to win legitimately, or Thinking plus Thief to cheat. However, he needs at least two successes to win, and may be rolling against another character or NPC.*

Extraordinarily difficult feats may need three successes; a good example would be leaping a motorcycle across the River Thames while singing the chorus from *The Ride of the*

Valkyries. However, such feats almost always require the use of more than one attribute, so more dice might be available. In this example Driving and Artist would be needed; the Mystic Power of levitation might also be useful...

Referee's Note: Encourage gratuitous attempts to use extra attributes provided that they are (a) described in suitably heroic terms by the player, (b) appropriate to the character and genre and (c) fun. This means that it is often easier to perform difficult and complex actions, which is absolutely right for this type of cinematic game! And of course Villains can do this too...

Optionally an easy unopposed roll that fails completely can be followed by a second attempt requiring a difficult roll (at least two successes needed) then by an extraordinarily difficult roll (three successes needed). Once there is even one success no more attempts may be made.

For important contests or combats (e.g., between one of the player characters and a major villain or god) the difference in the number of successes determines the result. For example, if Landmines and Diana fight, and Diana scores five successes while Landmines scores seven, Diana takes two hits (see below). If they both scored five hits they would block each other's blows, and neither would be hurt.

Ridiculously unbalanced matches should be determined by assuming that any successes that aren't used to achieve the desired result go on to affect the next man, the morale of the enemy, or whatever else seems appropriate. For example, if Diana is fighting a peasant army and her first blow scores eight successes the result is probably so spectacular that there is a good chance that anyone witnessing it will turn and run. Exactly what happens is left to the discretion of the referee (you were expecting elaborate morale rules?), who should determine the results by appropriateness to the genre. Usually players will have some idea of what they are trying to do, and the effect they expect to see: for example, "I'm going to grab the first peasant, tie him in a knot, and roll him at the rest like a bowling ball so they all go down.", "I'm going to chop his head off and try to get a few more with the follow-through", and so on.

Sometimes players will want to attack two or more separate foes; this is automatic against easy targets, as above, since any excess damage goes on to hit the next enemy. Against more challenging foes the character's Speed must equal or exceed that of the fastest opponent; if so, the number of dice available for the attack can be split as desired. This is a Difficult attack, with at least two successes needed to harm either opponent.

Example: *Using her Speed (4) and Martial Arts (7) combined, Diana wants to fight two ninjas. They have Speed (2), so Diana can do this; the player rolls 5D6 against one ninja, 6D6 against the other. She hits the first Ninja only once (a failure), the other five times (a success which knocks him out).*

Players may want to use a Martial Arts and Marksmanship attack in the same round; usually this will be along the lines of "I'll chop his head off with the sword and fire my crossbow at the guard..." Both weapons must be capable of being used simultaneously, only one attack can be given a bonus for a good or magical weapon (see below), and each attack must score at least two successes, but there is otherwise no problem.

Example: *Diana wants to use her sword and bow simultaneously—this isn't allowed, since she needs both hands for the bow.*

Example: *Wild Bill wants to shoot someone with his .44 Magnum and simultaneously kick a table into someone's face; this is allowed, he uses his Marksmanship plus a weapon bonus for the gun, his Martial Arts for the kick.*

If players want to use additional attributes (such as Speed or Athlete) they can do so if it seems appropriate to the genre, adding the dice for the attribute to either combat roll. Remember that they must describe what they are doing in graphic detail.

Example: *Diana back-flips onto the heads of a group of soldiers and starts to dance across the crowd, stomping their helmets while firing her bow at a more distant target. She uses Martial Arts plus Athlete to make the leap and kick the soldiers, Marksmanship plus a weapon bonus for the bow.*

Hit Points

Hit Points (usually called hits) represent the ability to withstand injury and fatigue. Each combat success that isn't absorbed by armour reduces hits by one. Injuries that don't reduce hits to zero have no effect except for a suitably dramatic-looking cut or bruise, possibly a spray of blood flicked by a sword or a grimace as an arrow is pulled out.

Unless there is some dramatic reason to do otherwise, all damage should be halved as soon as the scene ends, and should be healed completely after a night's sleep.

Example: *While fighting Landmines Diana takes six damage, reducing her hits to two. Between scenes three points of damage are removed, taking her to five hits. After a night's sleep she is back on her full eight hit points.*

Additionally, the Healing attribute allows its user to cure one hit for each success rolled. Only one attempt can be made to cure someone's injury, if it fails they are out of luck—but there may be another healer around, or the wounded person may just get better with time.

Sometimes it is dramatically essential for characters to suffer long-term injuries such as broken bones or a coma. Unless there is a good reason to do otherwise these characters should be on reduced hit points for the rest of the episode, and if unconscious play no direct part in the action (except perhaps as an out-of-body experience), but should make a full recovery for the next episode. If the injury occurs at the climax of an adventure it might be appropriate for the last scene to begin with friends signing the character's plaster cast, or with the character in a coma—the last line of the story can be "to be continued..." and the next episode can be the search for a cure.

If reduced to zero hit points the character is unconscious and/or dying, and low-status characters do indeed die as messily as possible. However, it is usually dramatically inappropriate for important people (such as the stars, villains, major henchmen and sidekicks) to die permanently, and something should always happen to ensure that the character is reincarnated in a miraculously restored body (or someone else's body), is replaced by a clone, replicant, or identical twin at the last moment, escapes through a trap door, or is simply knocked out or receives prompt first aid and gets better between scenes. Note that Villains in this genre are invariably subscribers to the "Before I kill you..." school; they will always aim to subdue their victims then subject them to elaborate (and invariably fallible) death traps.

To knock someone out without any risk of killing them the attacker should say that they are striking to knock out, not kill. Hit points are still lost, but the process ends with unconsciousness. All hit points are recovered when the victim wakes at a dramatically suitable moment.

Weapons

Weapons are used via Martial Arts or Marksmanship. A "normal" weapon (such as a small sword, nunchuks, a small hand-gun or rifle) is used without any modifiers to the attribute. More powerful or magical weapons (big swords, elephant rifles, mini-guns, etc.) may add to the number of dice rolled. Unusually weak or clumsy weapons may reduce it.

Example: *Landmines sometimes replaces his right hand with a Mini-Gun. When he fires it he rolls 11 dice for Marksmanship, not 8.*

Weapon	Dice	Weapon	Dice	Weapon	Dice
Spear	+1	Crossbow	+1	Small shotgun	-
Axe	+1	Small handgun	-	Large shotgun	+1
Dagger	-	Big handgun	+1	Machine pistol	+1
Sword	-	Huge handgun	+2	Submachine gun	+1
Big sword	+1	Small rifle	-	Machine gun	+2
Cricket ball	-1	Big rifle	+1	Mini gun	+3
Longbow	+2	Huge rifle	+2	Rotary cannon	+4

Weapon	Dice	Radius	Success
Hand grenade	5	5/10/15 ft	4+/5+/6
Dynamite	2 per stick	5/10/20 ft	4+/5+/6
Mortar shell	5	10/15/20 ft	4+/5+/6
Missile / torpedo	8	5/10/15 ft	4+/5+/6
Artillery / Bomb	10	10/20/30 ft	4+/5+/6
Land mine	8	10/15/20 ft	4+/5+/6
Car bomb	10	10/20/30 ft	4+/5+/6
Flame thrower	8	5/10/15 ft	4+/5+/6
Bagpipes	+3*	2/5/10 ft	4+/5+/6
	*added to Marksmanship skill		
Hydrogen bomb	25	1/2/5 miles	4+/5+/6

For guns, bows, and small projectiles such as throwing stars ammunition never runs out unless it's dramatically appropriate for it to do so, and range never seems to be important. Unless stated otherwise all hand weapons have a hit point plus one for each extra dice; thus a +2 sword has three hit points. Weapons are never damaged unless they are deliberately attacked.

When using multiple weapons (such as a sword and a knife) against a single target use the biggest bonus only; for example, if Fergie has a +1 knife and a +2 sword add only the +2 bonus. If attacking two or more targets as above, the highest bonus only is added to the total number of dice rolled.

Explosives and other area effect weapons such as flame-throwers have a number of dice listed, all targets within the radiuses shown are attacked by that many dice with the success numbers shown. A few examples of weapons and explosives are shown; others can easily be added.

Example: *Landmines' normal right hand is a disguised grenade. If he shakes hands with someone it will grab hold and drop from his wrist then explode a few seconds later, long enough for Landmines to get clear. The grenade attacks the victim and everyone else within range, rolling 5 dice for 4+ to hurt anyone within 5 ft., for 5+ to hurt anyone 5 to 10 ft. away, and for 6 to hurt anyone 10 to 15 ft. away.*

Weapons designed to stun (such as rubber bullets or stun grenades) have the same attack as their ordinary equivalents but cause unconsciousness rather than permanent injuries.

Magical weapons can add to attributes, as above, or add some unique capability.

Example: *Diana's sword (which may possibly be Excalibur) adds +3 to Martial Arts in her hands only and disrupts some forms of magic (determined by the referee). It also returns to her hand if it is thrown.*

Armour

Armour absorbs some of the damage from an attack. Lightweight armour such as motorcycle leathers or a chainmail bikini absorbs the first hit of an attack. Heavier armour such as Kevlar absorbs the first two hits. Unless the referee rules otherwise it will not be damaged by the attack. Vehicle armour and buildings can absorb more damage, but any hits which penetrate destroy the armour.

Example: *Landmines dresses in Kevlar. The first two hits of each attack are absorbed without damaging the armour. This is recorded as Armour, -2 hits.*

Example: *A tank has steel armour absorbing up to 5 hits. If it takes more damage than that the armour is destroyed, and any left-over hits go on to damage the occupants.*

Other Ouchies

Normally combat will be the main source of injuries in a campaign, but occasionally someone will fall off a cliff, get run over, or otherwise go in harm's way. The golden rule here is that it is seldom dramatically appropriate to kill a major character in this way; injure yes, kill no. For most circumstances no more than 50% of hit points should be lost; if this means falling from orbit and taking only 3 points of damage then the player or referee needs to explain it ("fortunately I was wearing heatproof boots") or find some other way out ("OK, you hurtle from orbit towards the ground. As the next scene begins you are sitting at the bar of a friendly tavern, covered in scratches and bits of broken twig, and have just said 'You won't believe the day I've been having...' when four of Thatcher's goons burst through the door...").

Occasionally it is dramatically appropriate for someone to take a serious injury in these circumstances, as described above. Spending an episode in a coma or a plaster cast is the most likely result. Death should only occur if it is dramatically appropriate, if there really is no way out, and in circumstances that leave some possibility of resurrection or a return, if only in flashback.

Example: *The adventurers are thrown into Thatcher's "giant spikey garbage crusher of doom" death trap, and Red Ken heroically holds the walls apart long enough for Diana and Fergie to escape. But in doing so Red Ken is repeatedly injured, and the trap slams closed to squash him. By the time the others get it open there's nothing left but a bloody corpse. Eventually Diana and Co. prepare to give it a Viking funeral on the Thames, but a horde of frogs and toads drives them back before they can start the fire. When they fight them off the body is gone. Months pass... then the remaining adventurers are somehow led to a pond containing a gigantic amphibian's egg, a pod in which Red Ken's body has slowly regenerated.*

Mystic Powers

Mystic Powers can range from silly (Diana's always-pristine clothing) to spectacular—levitation, bolts of energy, mind control and the like. Powers that affect the world or other characters usually function like the nearest equivalent attribute, or attack an attribute. Mystic Powers must always be agreed by the player and referee.

Example: *Elizabeth's mind control ability uses her Mystic Power to attack her victim's Thinking and Mystic Power attribute combined. When she uses it against a player character both should roll the appropriate attributes; if Elizabeth rolls more successes she takes control of the victim's mind, otherwise her power is resisted. If she uses it against an extra she should almost always succeed.*

Example: *Elizabeth's energy power works like the blast of an energy weapon, attacking hit points, but can only be resisted by Mystic Power.*

Example: *Diana's superhuman accuracy with her bow lets her add her Mystic Power to her Marksmanship for difficult shots, such as ricochetsand very small targets. This requires extra time to concentrate, so she cannot use the power in normal combat.*

Character Development

Each character should have a Back Story which relates the character to the star and at least two or three NPCs. For example, Red Ken's Back Story involves Diana, Fergie, Thatcher the Sorceress and Archer the Assassin. The Back Story should mention any unusual or unique talent, such as Fergie's tracking or Red Ken's ability to understand reptiles and amphibians, and must be agreed with the referee.

Costs of Status Improvement	
Status	**Cost (BP)**
0-19	10
20-49	15
50+ or Star	20

Character Development is achieved by raising Status. The referee should award bonus points for suitably over-the-top acting, creative use of attributes and Mystic Powers, or anything else that seems appropriate. Players may spend the points to improve Status (for the costs shown to the right), each improvement in Status allows one attribute to be raised (to a maximum of 10). Hit points should be adjusted to reflect

Status. Try to avoid giving more than 5-10 points per character in a single episode.

❀If the Status of the Star reaches 50 it is likely that the game will become very unbalanced, with the star monopolising most scenes. This is probably a cue to think about starting a new series.

❀If the Status of co-stars exceeds 40 they are ready to become stars in their own right, and the referee should consider developing a spin-off series starring the character.

❀The referee can decrease Status if a character is played in a way that contradicts the Back Story. For example, Diana's Back Story makes it clear that she defends the innocent, especially children. If Diana kills an innocent, regardless of circumstances, her Status immediately falls. Attributes aren't lost if Status falls, but hit points are. Any really severe lapse should be punished more harshly; for example, if Diana wiped out an entire orphanage deliberately she would become a villainess; the referee might also consider removing her Mystic Power and magic sword, since she is now unworthy of them.

❀Temporary losses of Status make the character tired, old, and wrinkled without killing them. It's often dramatically appropriate to reduce attributes too. All should be fully restored if the loss is replaced.

Unspent bonus points may instead be used to boost any attribute for a single use; for example, Diana might spend three points to add three dice to her Martial Arts in the first blow when fighting Landmines, God of War.

Optionally points may be used for other purposes. For example, the referee might let a player spend several points for a plot development that will favour their character, such as the acquisition of a magical weapon or the opportunity to be the main star of an episode.

Example: *The referee introduces a cute kid to the campaign. After several episodes a player pays a few points for a plot development that will get rid of the scene-stealing brat.*

NPCs

NPCs range from major villains such as Landmines and Thatcher to Status 1 peasants. For these lesser mortals it probably isn't necessary to keep detailed character records; for most purposes all that is likely to be needed is a name, details of combat capabilities, and possibly one or two other attributes and notes on equipment carried. Similarly, animals and other inhuman NPCs should be defined in terms of their hit points, armour, and any relevant attributes. For these creatures the Martial Arts attribute may be replaced with a more specialised attack such as Bite, Claws, Crush, Kick. In a few cases (such as venomous snakes) there are two forms of attack, the second only occurring if the first succeeds, and possibly having different success numbers. For example, a cobra is recorded as Bite/venom 3/6 dice, 6/5 success, meaning that it bites with three dice with a success number of 6 but uses six dice for its venom with a success number of 5+ if the bite does damage. The table below lists some typical NPCs, animals, and other things that might be useful:

Typical Peasant *Attack:* Martial Arts (1) *Success:* 6 *Hits:* 1 *Notes:* Strength (2), Healing (2) or other non-combat attributes. Rake or other improvised weapon.

Cannon Fodder *Attack:* Martial Arts (1), Marksmanship (1) *Success:* 6 *Hits:* 1 *Notes:* Strength (2), Rifle.

Typical Soldier *Attack:* Martial Arts (2), Marksmanship (3) *Success:* 6 *Hits:* 1 *Notes:* Strength (1), Rifle +1

Typical Sergeant *Attack:* Martial Arts (3), Marksmanship (3) *Success:* 6 *Hits:* 2 *Notes:* Strength (2), Speed (2), Machine gun +2, knife, grenades.

Scorpion *Attack:* Sting (2)/Venom (3) *Success:* 6/5 *Hits:* 1 *Notes:* Typically encountered in swarms in dungeon scorpion pits or alone in the desert.

Rat *Attack:* Bite (1) *Success:* 6 *Hits:* 1 *Notes:* Rats attack in large swarms, e.g. 2D6 per adventurer.

Cat *Attack:* Scratch (1) *Success:* 6 *Hits:* 2 *Notes:* Speed (2). A typical household cat, usually friendly.

Dog *Attack:* Bite (2) *Success:* 6 *Hits:* 3 *Notes:* Speed (2). A large dog, e.g. a guard dog.

Lion *Attack:* Bite (4), Claws (4) *Success:* 5 *Hits:* 6 *Notes:* Speed (4). Can use claws, bite, or both simultaneously.

Rattlesnake *Attack:* Bite (2)/Venom (5) *Success:* 6/5 *Hits:* 3 *Notes:* Speed (2). A typical rattlesnake.

Cobra *Attack:* Bite (2)/Venom (5) *Success:* 6/5 *Hits:* 3 *Notes:* Speed (1). A large cobra.

Boa Constrictor *Attack:* Bite (2)/Crush (6) *Success:* 6/5 *Hits:* 5 *Notes:* Strength (3). A large boa constrictor.

Alligator *Attack:* Bite (6) *Success:* 6 *Hits:* 8 *Notes:* Strength (4), Armoured -2 all attacks.

Horse *Attack:* Kick (5) *Success:* 5 *Hits:* 6 *Notes:* Speed (4), Strength (4).

Elephant *Attack:* Trample (6) *Success:* 5 *Hits:* 8 *Notes:* Speed (3), Strength (6), Thinking (2).

Shark *Attack:* Bite (7) *Success:* 6 *Hits:* 7 *Notes:* Speed (4).

Giant Octopus *Attack:* Crush (6) *Success:* 5 *Hits:* 6 *Notes:* Thinking (1). Can attack several targets simultaneously.

Dolphin *Attack:* Bite (3) *Success:* 6 *Hits:* 3 *Notes:* Speed (5), Thinking (2). Often friendly.

Killer Whale *Attack:* Bite (8) *Success:* 5 *Hits:* 10 *Notes:* Speed (5), Thinking (3). Often friendly.

Golem *Attack:* Grab (4)/Crush (8) *Success:* 6/5 *Hits:* 10 *Notes:* Thinking (1), Strength (6). Armoured -3 all attacks. May be unusually susceptible to Mystic Power.

Robot *Attack:* Punch (8)/Marksmanship (5) *Success:* 6 *Hits:* 10 *Notes:* Thinking (2), Strength (5). Armoured -2 all attacks, may have guns and other weapons built in.

Zombie *Attack:* Bite (2)/Disease (4) *Success:* 6/5 *Hits:* 4 *Notes:* Thinking (1), Strength (2). May be unusually susceptible to Mystic Power.

Grey Alien *Attack:* Martial Arts (3)/Marksmanship (5) *Success:* 5 *Hits:* 5 *Notes:* Thinking (6), Science (6), Mystic Power (4), Ray gun +3.

Gadgets

Gadgets range from the mundane cell-phones and CD players described above to elaborate engines of destruction. Regrettably it's highly likely that characters will have more to do with engines of destruction than anything else. What follows is necessarily a brief overview, and referees should feel free to elaborate on these descriptions or add more items as they see fit. Unless stated otherwise all gadgets catch fire and burn if reduced to zero hit points, even things that appear to be completely non-flammable. Most electrical equipment shorts out and burns if it gets wet.

Type	Armour	Hits
Laptop	-	1
Desktop	-1	2-4
Mainframe	-2	5-10
AI*	-3	5-10
*Thinking (1D6)		

Computers are programmed by punched card (the biggest also have paper tape); nevertheless there are laptop, office, and mainframe machines. The standard punched card is about the size of a postcard, with thousands of tiny perforations. On a laptop it slots into the side below the keyboard. Only one card is needed per program, regardless of complexity. The user interface is via the keyboard and touching the screen.

Artificial intelligence exists but is very rare and seen only on the largest machines (notable for big reels of paper tape that look like player piano rolls); cutting the tape is one way to defeat an AI, another is to pose a logic problem such as "Why?"[9]. If an AI is defeated it will crash and burn (literally).

The casings of larger computers are generally made of steel plate with lots of rivets, inside there are elaborate arrangements of rotating cams and gears, valves and flashing lights. Laptop PCs are roughly briefcase-sized, usually with wooden casings which tend to have elaborate filigree inlay and marquetry. They short-circuit (with impressive sparks, smoke, and flames) if they get wet. All programs apart from games have lots of pull-down menus in a largely text-based interface, with an occasional screen of graphics.

---

9. Unfortunately Really smart AIs say "Why not?" and carrying on working.

Civilian Vehicles

Civilian Vehicles come in a huge variety of styles and designs, with power sources ranging from steam to internal combustion to nuclear propulsion. Nevertheless they can be divided into a few broad classes with roughly similar performance.

All but the smallest ground vehicles have effectively unlimited load capacity. Most road vehicles move at about 50 MPH; high performance designs such as sports cars and motorbikes move at 80 MPH. For game purposes ordinary cars move at Speed 3, high performance cars at Speed 5 if someone is trying to out-run them. All except bikes provide armour to their occupants; if reduced to zero hits they crash, catch fire, and explode three rounds later. They also catch fire and explode three rounds later if they crash for other reasons. All can operate on or off the road.

Ships and boats start at about 20 MPH (Speed 1), with high-speed craft such as hovercraft and hydrofoils reaching 40-50 MPH (speed 3), and seem to have unlimited capacity. Their sides usually provide some armour. Usually they catch fire and/or explode before sinking. Oddly the external appearance of a ship often bears little resemblence to its interior; for example, a tramp steamer or a submarine might have a cabin designed for a Spanish galleon. Holds seem to be especially stretchy if it suits the needs of the plot; in one play-test most of the contents of London Zoo fitted into a single barge. Most ships run heavily to rivets, brass pipes and boilers and a general 19th century look even if nuclear powered. They are steered using the Driving skill; navigation is never a problem unless it is dramatically appropriate.

Aircraft range from blimps and hang-gliders to helicopters, jets, and space shuttles, some of them steam powered. Most are too fast for anyone on foot to keep up with them, and seem to have no problem carrying massive loads. Many are amphibious, landing on water as easily as on land. Like boats and ships, the interiors of all but the smallest planes are malleable for the needs of the plot. For example, an aircraft that looks like a Ford Trimotor on the outside might have a swimming pool or a jacuzzi inside. It may also sound like a jet. Helicopters and some other aircraft are capable of VTOL flight.

Aircraft (up to and including space shuttles) are flown using the Driving skill; navigation is never a problem unless it is dramatically appropriate. If they are reduced to zero hit points and have a player character aboard they start to dive and eventually crash, giving ample time to get to an exit; if there is nobody "important" aboard they either crash at a dramatically appropriate point or explode. Most aircraft carry parachutes for their passengers, but there are never enough for everyone aboard. If it becomes necessary to use them there will invariably be a cute kid, an injured nun, or a kitten left aboard when the parachutes run out. Space shuttles carry space suits instead (see below); again, there are never quite enought for the number of people needing them.

There are pirate aircraft which prey on civilian craft; they are armed with cannon and typically use radios to order the pilot of the craft they are attacking to fly a steady course, blow a hole through the hull using the cannon (decompression isn't a problem in this world), then lock the aircraft together using powerful magnets and board through the hole. Pirates are usually armed with cutlasses and pistols. Statistics are provided below.

Space shuttles routinely fly to orbit, where NASA (Norton's Agency for Space Achievement) is preparing for the first Lunar expedition. See the episode outlines above for more on this.

Type	Speed	Armour	Hits
Motorbike	80 MPH	-	4
Small car	50	-1	6
Sports car	80	-2	6
Bus	30	-2	10
Truck	40	-2	15
Jet ski	30	-	4
Motorboat	30	-1	6
Paddle Steamer	20	-2	15
Liner/freighter	30	-2	25
Bulk carrier	20	-2	40
Hang glider	50 MPH	-	2
Blimp	50	-	5
Biplane	100	-1	5
Helicopter	150	-1	10
Prop transport	200	-1	10
Executive jet	500	-1	10
Airliner	500	-2	15
SST	1500	-2	15
Space Shuttle	5000	-3	20

Military Vehicles

Military Vehicles are much like their civilian equivalents, but usually better armoured. Their game function is usually to be a target of the adventurers attacks, so most seem to be remarkably flimsy. It is entirely possible to cut through the armour of a tank with a sword! Once the armour is penetrated by an attack, all subsequent attacks go on to harm the vehicle (if occupied by important NPCs or adventurers) or its occupants (if minor NPCs); when a fighting vehicle is destroyed or the crew are killed it catches fire (even if underwater) and explodes a few rounds later.

Type	Speed	Armour	Hits	Weapons and Notes
Motorbike	60 MPH	-	5	None, or machine gun in side car.
Jeep/land rover	50	-1	10	Machine gun.
Field gun	See note	-1	10	Cannon(firing artillery shells). Speed as towing vehicle.
Armoured car	50	-4	15	Machine gun or mini gun.
Tank	30	-5	20	Cannon, Rotary cannon.
Mecha	60	-4	20	2 Rotary cannon, 8 missiles, Strength (8), Martial Arts +5 (to max. 10).
Military Blimp	50	-	5	4 bombs, 2 machine guns.
Attack helicopter	200	-2	10	2 Rotary cannon, 4 missiles, VTOL
Biplane fighter	100	-1	5	2 Machine guns
Jet fighter	1500	-2	15	Rotary cannon, 8 missiles, VTOL
Pirate aircraft	400	-2	15	(a modified airliner) Cannon, 4 machine guns, powerful magnets.
Jet bomber	500	-2	20	8 Bombs, 8 missiles
Flying dreadnaught	75	-2	25	4 cannon, 8 Rotary cannon, 8 missile launchers, lots of missiles and bombs

More Military Vehicles

Type	Speed	Armour	Hits	Weapons and Notes
Small warship	40	-3	20	2 cannon, 8 Rotary cannon
Large warship	30	-3	30	8 cannon, 16 Rotary cannon, 8 missile launchers, lots of missiles
Submarine	30	-5	20	16 long-range missiles (nuclear warheads), 4 torpedoes (as missiles)

Vehicle weapons are usually used with the Marksmanship and Speed of the driver/pilot or gunner. Machine guns and rotary cannon are used normally, larger weapons such as cannon (a loose term which refers to all guns firing artillery shells, regardless of size), flame throwers and missile launchers are fired using the gunner's Marksmanship, but do damage according to the explosive rules above if they hit the target.

Mecha can also use Martial Arts provided the driver can; the Mecha's +5 is added to the driver's attribute, to a maximum of Martial Arts 10. If the driver has no Martial Arts this capability cannot be used, the controls are too tricky and the mecha falls over.

Flying Dreadnaughts are essentially flying warships with dozens of propellers holding them aloft, invented by Prince Albert Einstein; they are slow (in combat they manoeuvre and fire after all other craft, regardless of their speed in miles per hour) but can hover over an enemy and attack with bombs, missiles, and other weapons. They can only land on water.

Other Equipment

Most other equipment should be described to fit the needs of the plot, with lots of twiddly bits, dials, brass, and rivets. Sometimes the function should be somewhat different from the equivalent in our world. Remember that while these descriptions may seem odd to players, the characters should take them for granted. Here are a few examples:

Action figures: Many of those living in this superstitious age carry small religious icons called "Action figures". These are little manniquins about 3" tall, often with jointed arms and legs, some resembling humans, others demons of one sort or another such as Old Nick O'Teen or dread Jajabinks. These are used for prayer ceremonies and ritual magic. Note that some are genuinely magical, acting as a focus for Mystic Power in the right hands. 1 hit.

Aqualung: Two heavy brass gas bottles linked to a brass diver's helmet. The bottles hold enough air for several hours, there are never problems about decompression times or the bends. 3 hits.

Books: Books are printed with hand-set type and hand-drawn illuminations, and are invariably massive leather-bound volumes. 1 hit.

Camera: A wood and brass box fitted with bellows, a motor drive, and electronic flash. Pictures are usually self-developing colour prints. 1 hit.

First aid kit: Contains a jar of leeches, some bandages and tape, various leaves and herbs used as painkillers or to cure various diseases (in cellophane packets), and a vial of mouldy bread labelled as "penicillin". Adds +1 dice to Healing. 1 hit.

Guitar: All guitars (even those used by primitive savages or in areas without power supplies) look like Fender Stratocasters and have built in amplification and effects. 2 hits.

Microscope: Invariably made of brass with two eyepieces, they can see bacteria, viruses and large molecules. The image is always crystal clear, sharp, and bright, even if the microscope is illuminated by a flickering oil lamp. Microscopes give +1 dice to any relevant Science or Healing roll. 1 hit.

Space suit: These come in two versions:

1) Bulky white vacuum suits, with manoeuvring jets and some armour (-2 hits) built in, worn by Norton's astronauts and most "serious" space explorers. They look like NASA suits of the 1960s/70s and have 4 hits.

2) Thin garments made out of clinging clear plastic with a goldfish-bowl helmet, backpack, and belt with little jet nozzles. These seem to be reserved for female space pirates who invariably strip to minimal underwear before putting one on. Presumably the cooling systems don't work too well... They have no armour (except possibly a chain-mail bikini), 2 hits.

For both types of suits, any damage which gets past the armour and destroys the suit should be treated as decompressing the suit. Minor NPCs invariably panic, swell up and explode; Villains and adventurers have time to find the puncture repair kit first.

A repaired suit has no hit points or armour and will leak slowly, but there should be just time to get to an airlock before air runs out.

Telescope: A brass tube about a foot long extending to 2-3 feet. Gyrostabilisation, image intensification, and thermal imaging are built in. 1 hit.

Television: TVs look like triple-lensed magic lantern projectors; the picture is projected onto a sheet of ground glass held in an adjustable frame. Images usually have coloured fringes at the edges. They have twin spiral antennae with a Jacob's Ladder effect. Some work as two-way picture phones, with a dial and candle-stick receiver. They have no armour, one hit point, and catch fire if damaged. Video recorders look like old-style cylinder phonographs without the horn, and connect to the TV via an armoured metal hose. 1 hit.

Tuba: An acoustic weapon with the same weapon stats as bagpipes. 2 hits.

Space Suit: Thin garments made out of clinging clear plastic with a goldfish-bowl helmet, backpack, and belt with little jet nozzles. These seem to be reserved for female space pirates who invariably strip to minimal underwear before putting one on. Presumably the cooling systems don't work too well...

Principal Characters

The following section contains game data for the main heroes and villains of the Diana universe. If players take on these roles they should be given copies of the appropriate record. A blank character record is also provided below.

Name:

Status:

Success: Armour: Hit Points:

Bonus Points:

Attributes

Animal Handler: Marksmanship:

Artist: Martial Arts:

Athlete: Mystic Power:

Charisma: Speed:

Computers: Strength:

Driving: Thief:

Healing: Thinking:

Luck:

Quote:

Back Story:

Diana, Warrior Princess

Status: 40 (star)
Success: 5+
Armour: -1
Hit Points: 8
Bonus Points:
Attributes:
  Animal
        Handler (3)
  Athlete (4)
  Charisma (4)
  Driving (3)
  Luck (2)
  Marksmanship (4)
  Martial Arts (7)
  Mystic Power (5)
  Speed (4)
  Strength (3)
  Thinking (1)

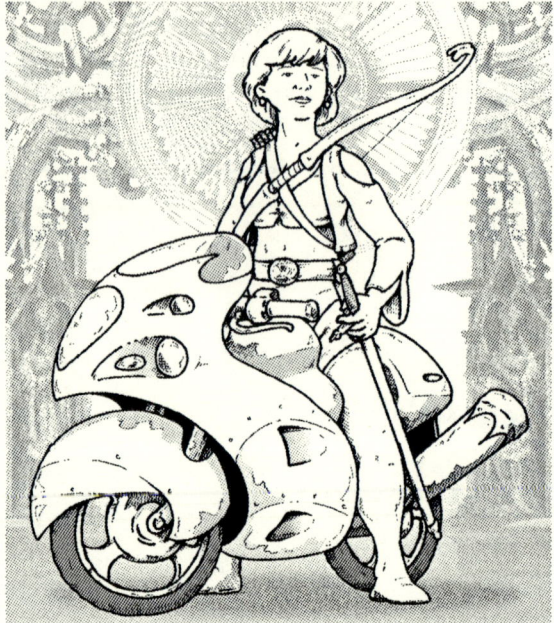

Quote: "I'll bring peace to this land if it kills us all..."

Back Story: Diana was an "ordinary" Princess until she began to suspect that her husband, Bonnie Prince Charlie, was unfaithful. While seeking evidence she discovered his involvement in a hideous black-market trade in arms and the deadly drug "tobacco", both sold to children in third-world countries, and responsibility for the deaths of thousands of innocents.

Diana immediately denounced and divorced him. Somehow she retained the Mystic Powers of Royalty after the divorce, despite being Royal by marriage, not birth, while Prince Charlie lost them. She has since dedicated her life to Peace, fighting war (and the war-god Landmines) whenever she encounters it. Somehow this dedication gives her superhuman strength and speed. This behaviour has earned her the enmity of Queen Elizabeth, who wishes to silence her permanently. She has since escaped from kidnapping and assassination attempts, but must be wary whenever she is in England. Landmines also wants to stop her, but hopes that he might be able to "turn" her to his side.

Her best friends are Fergie, her constant companion, and Red Ken, a barbarian hero. Ken is a little too ready to use violence but his heart is definitely in the right place. She is also reasonably friendly with Wild Bill Gates, a riverboat gambler and occasional con-man who has helped her on several occasions. Prince Charlie occasionally turns up to make a nuisance of himself. Another occasional nuisance is Ron L. Hubble, a slimy fraudster.

Possessions: A powerful motorbike which behaves much like a horse; for example, if Diana leaps off to fight someone it will slow, circle back, and stop (with the engine running) somewhere convenient for Diana to leap back on. White low-cut motorcycle leathers which are always spotlessly clean, even if she has just waded through mud or a bloodbath. Camping and cooking gear and some changes of clothing in the motorcycle panniers (which seem to have implausibly huge capacity). She always has plenty of money, usually in gold coins. A cell-phone.

Diana's Motorbike: 10 Hits, Armour -2, Speed (6), Thinking (1). Unlike most vehicles it doesn't explode if it crashes.

Weapons: Diana's main weapons are her incredibly accurate longbow (+3 when used by Diana only), and her magic sword (+3, returns to her hands when thrown, appears to deflect or disrupt some forms of magic) which may possibly be Excalibur, nobody is entirely sure. Needless to say her hands and feet are lethal weapons, and she can use her Mystic Powers to boost her martial arts and marksmanship (see notes). Nevertheless Diana will always try to disarm or knock out her opponents, to do this simply tell the referee that you are fighting to disarm or stun, not kill. Diana's leathers act as armour, absorbing the first hit of any attack.

Notes: Diana's Mystic Powers of Royalty protect her clothing from dirt ("How do you know she's a princess?" "She isn't covered in shit...") and allow her to heal some diseases by laying on her hands (replacing the Healing attribute), but their main effect is to boost her combat and athletic capabilities, speed, and strength, but only in unusually difficult situations. She needs at least one round without combat to meditate and achieve this heightened mystical state, once she has done so she can combine the attributes. Her Mystic Powers can also boost her charisma.

Fergie

Status: 35 (co-star)
Success: 5+
Armour: -1
Hit Points: 7
Bonus Points:
Attributes:
  Animal Handler (3)
  Athlete (5)
  Charisma (2)
  Driving (1)
  Healing (3)
  Marksmanship (5)
  Martial Arts (5)
  Speed (3)
  Strength (3)
  Thief (2)
  Thinking (3)

  Quote: "I don't know, one of his enemies must have caught up with him..."

  Back Story: Fergie is Diana's sidekick, a country girl of good (but vaguely defined) background who has somehow attached herself to the Warrior Princess. She is superficially a dumb redhead, has a heart of gold, and is very good with children and animals. Appearances can be deceptive; she is much smarter than she looks, a competent martial artist, and an expert hunter and tracker. She kills if she feels it is necessary, and does so fairly often; while she respects Diana's goals, she occasionally disposes of enemies that Diana would leave alive, if she thinks she can do so without Diana finding out.

  Fergie likes Red Ken the barbarian, tolerates Wild Bill Gates (he's fun and reasonably reliable in a fight), mildly dislikes Bonnie Prince Charlie (if he wasn't such a wimp she'd detest him, but it's obvious that he's totally under his mother's thumb), and loathes Ron L. Hubble (he's scum and she'll kill him if she

is sure she can do it without Diana or anyone else noticing, but it isn't high priority).

Possessions: Fergie seems to have few or no possessions other than the clothes she wears (usually a heavy quilted jacket over a long slit skirt and heavy boots; remarkably this clothing does not hamper her movements), and occasional off-road cars or horses which she seems to acquire and lose without explanation—she probably borrows them. She has a cell-phone and a first aid kit (containing bandages, leeches, penicillin, etc.), adds +1 to healing.

Weapons: Fergie carries a big sword (+1) and at least two concealed knives at all times. These have no Mystic Power, they're just sharp. She has also used firearms but doesn't habitually carry them. Her quilted jacket acts as armour, absorbing the first hit of an attack, but its protection is destroyed after the first hit until it is repaired.

Notes: Fergie is remarkably unlucky and is the most likely candidate to be bitten by a vampire, venomous snake or radioactive spider, kidnapped, hypnotised, enchanted, or abducted by aliens. She can always track footprints etc. by making a Thinking roll (+2 dice for this special ability only).

Red Ken, Barbarian Hero

Status: 25
  (guest star)
Success: 5+
Hit Points: 5
Bonus Points:
Attributes:
  Animal Handler (6)
  Athlete (3)
  Charisma (2)
  Luck (2)
  Marksmanship (3)
  Martial Arts (3)
  Speed (3)
  Strength (3)

Quote: (looks at a frog making "gurkk" noises) "My little friends tell me that there is a stranger in these woods..."

Back Story: Red Ken is a barbarian hero who aims to free London from the rule of the sorceress Thatcher, who rules the city and bleeds its citizens of their wealth and freedom. Thatcher's most deadly assassin, the enigmatic Archer, is on his trail but has so far failed to kill him. Red Ken is a skilled martial artist and knife-thrower, but his main expertise is with animals; he can ride superbly, and his pet lizards, salamanders, frogs and snakes seem to obey his very thoughts and have saved Diana or Fergie's life on several occasions. Diana doesn't entirely approve of Ken, since he believes that Thatcher's crimes justify the use of lethal force, but there are ambiguous hints that they have at some stage been lovers. There are also hints that he and Fergie have been lovers, or that all three have shared some sort of relationship. He seems to be more of a member of the "team" than Diana's other allies. He is a friendly rival of Wild Bill Gates, but regards

Bonnie Prince Charlie as a wimp and Ron L. Hubble as slime.

Possessions: Red Ken usually rides a powerful war-horse, and carries various frogs, toads, reptiles and snakes in a leather pouch, shoulder bag, or saddle bags. A few changes of clothing (leather trousers and a green jerkin, no armour protection). A fishing line and hooks, snares, and other hunting/poaching equipment.

Weapons: Eight throwing knives hidden in sleeves, boots, and clothing. Nunchuks (+1). Dozens of throwing stars—Ken never seems to run out.

Notes: Ken has a unique talent, the ability to communicate with reptiles and amphibians if he makes an Animal Handling roll. There is nothing in his Back Story so far to explain it. Maybe he was turned into a newt but got better...

Wild Bill Gates, Riverboat Gambler

Status: 25
  (guest star)
Success: 5+
Hit Points: 5
Bonus Points:
Attributes:
  Athlete (1)
  Computers (3)
  Charisma (2)
  Driving (1)
  Luck (3)
  Marksmanship (3)
  Martial Arts (1)
  Science (1)
  Speed (4)
  Thief (3)
  Thinking (3)

Quote: "I didn't say the land I sold you was above water..."

Back Story: Wild Bill Gates is a river-boat gambler and entrepreneur who tends to turn up with dubious schemes whenever the action moves to America, and occasionally takes his schemes to other countries. He is often seen running from angry mobs. He is a skilled gambler, quick-draw gunfighter, and occasionally competent computer programmer (using punched cards and tape, of course), famous for his slogan "Make Money Fast". He is a loyal ally of Diana, with suggestions he would like to be a good deal more, and will reluctantly risk his life to save her. He is a friendly rival of Red Ken but regards Bonnie Prince Charlie as a wimp and Ron L. Hubble as slime.

Possessions: Several packs of playing cards (some marked), also punch cards, paper tape, and other programming equipment. A laptop computer. He has on several occasions appeared to be the owner of a riverboat (a different boat each time), but it's possible that they were borrowed or stolen.

Weapons: A .44 magnum automatic (+2) and two tiny concealed pistols. No armour.

Notes: A useful role model is Brett Maverick.

Bonnie Prince Charlie

Status: 20 (guest star)
Success: 5+
Hit Points: 4
Bonus Points:
Attributes:
 Animal Handler (2)
 Artist (2)
 Athlete (2)
 Charisma (1)
 Driving (3)
 Luck (1)
 Marksmanship (4)
 Martial Arts (2)
 Speed (1)
 Strength (1)
 Thinking (1)

 Quote: "I say, Diana, couldn't we... you know... get together again?"

 Back Story: Bonnie Prince Charlie is Diana's ex-husband. He isn't a bad person but is easily led and extremely suggestible, frequently mind-controlled by his mother, who can see through his eyes and take over his body at will; this is signalled by his eyes changing colour, by a change in speech and stance, and by the use of horrific casual violence. He collapses afterwards. Diana and Fergie are not aware of this evil; somehow it always happens when neither is in a position to observe him, and they (and he) always assume that someone must have knocked him out. He has no Mystic Powers of Royalty; before his divorce he occasionally experienced brief flashes of this force, but they seem to have deserted him completely now.

 He can fly jets and helicopters, ride a horse, and shoots reasonably well. He should be played as comic relief when in his own mind, turning up to pester Diana with flowers, paintings (his main artistic talent) and other gifts in an attempt to persuade her to remarry him, at the most awkward possible moment.

Often these gifts are prompted by his mother and contain traps for Diana; for example, a jewelled pendant might be cursed, stolen from someone extremely powerful, or contain a bug or a small bomb. He tries to help Diana, but his clumsiness and his mother's influence usually means that it all ends in tears. He is vaguely aware that Diana and Fergie have friends such as Red Ken, Wild Bill Gates, and Ron L. Hubble (who recently sold the Prince some very promising-looking shares in a pharmaceuticals company that is about to announce a cure for Lepus) but rarely gives them much thought.

Possessions: The Prince is fabulously wealthy and always seems to have a new car, plane, airship, etc. He usually wears a tiny lop-sided crown over a business suit. He has a cell-phone.

Weapons: Usually carries a shotgun (+1) in his luggage, most of his aircraft and some of his cars are equipped with concealed weaponry, installed secretly by Elizabeth's hench-men; he doesn't know that the weapons have been installed, but Elizabeth can use them when she controls his mind. No armour.

Notes: When in his own mind Charlie is vague and inoffensive; when overcome by Elizabeth he is forceful and dynamic, and his Martial arts, Marksmanship, and Strength rise; exactly how much they rise depends on how hard Elizabeth is trying.

Ron L. Hubble, Con-man

Status: 20 (guest star)
Success: 5+
Hit Points: 4
Bonus Points:
Attributes:
  Artist (1)
  Charisma (1)
  Computers (1)
  Driving (1)
  Luck (1)
  Marksmanship (1)
  Martial Arts (1)
  Science (2)
  Speed (2)
  Strength (1)
  Thief (5)
  Thinking (3)

Quote: "OK, so the diet pills contained tapeworm eggs. People lost weight, didn't they?"

Back Story: Hubble is a blatant con-man. Most of his rackets, such as a "miracle radiation cure" based on molasses, involve an element of pseudo-science. He is most notorious for selling NASA (Norton's Agency for Space Achievement) a space telescope designed so badly that it had to be fitted with spectacles. He is on the run from at least one warlord's assassins. He will always try to scuttle away from combat if possible, preferably manipulating Diana or some other hero to do his fighting for him.

Diana has saved his life on two occasions, but also interfered with some of his most creative cons. If he can ever get her to endorse one of his schemes he'll undoubtedly make a fortune. Fergie is just a dim bimbo, conning her ought to be easy. Red Ken is a dangerous nut; anyone who keeps toads in his belt pouch is seriously strange, and what's more one of them bit Ron the last time he tried to check out the pouch. Wild Bill Gates is dangerous too—he's as big a crook as Ron is, and a much better shot, and has somehow persuaded Diana that he's on her side. Bonnie Prince Charlie is the dream mark for every con-man that ever lived; Ron has sold him shares in a non-existent company that's allegedly working on a cure for Lepus (there is no cure other than the Mystic Power of Royalty, of course), and would like to do more business with him, but his mother is very bad news so he's being cautious.

Possessions: A luxury limousine, some bags of gold (including a bag of faked coins, gold-plated lead), several phoney medical, legal, and scientific diplomas, and a medical bag full of nostrums such as snake oil, laudanum, and anti-virus software. He usually has a few fake gadgets with him; most notably, a gizmo which is supposed to detect the Mystic Powers of Royalty—it's obviously defective since it doesn't detect them in Prince Charlie. A cell-phone.

Weapons: A small pistol and a rifle (+1) in his car.

Notes: Hubble is slime, always scheming and looking for a quick profit, without any concern for the consequences. If he was better organised he'd probably become a seriously dangerous Villain, but it's too much like hard work.

Landmines, God of War

Status: 50 (God)
Success: 4+
Armour: -2
Hit Points: 10
Bonus Points:
Attributes:
  Animal
       Handler (2)
  Athlete (4)
  Charisma (4)
  Driving (2)
  Marksmanship (8)
  Martial Arts (8)
  Mystic Power (8)
  Science (2)
  Speed (5)
  Strength (5)
  Thinking (2)

Quote: "You have failed me, but I am moved and even slightly amused by your grovelling. Here, take my hand..."

Back Story: Landmines, God of War is a half-man, half-machine hybrid, brutally attractive, who incorporates numerous weapons into his body. His right hand is made of metal; a regular series joke consists of him saying "let me give you a hand", or variants thereof, giving it to a victim who is seized by it then engulfed in flames as it explodes. He will never kill Diana, but makes frequent attempts to "turn" her, usually by tricking her into killing an innocent. He then plans to make her his mistress, and transform her into the unstoppable magical cyborg of his dreams. Landmines can be killed, but since he is a god he always returns. He usually appears as the dark power behind a warlord or some act of oppression, or plotting to stir up violence and chaos.

Possessions: Any military hardware he wants. He can vanish at will and reappear carrying weapons, or with them replacing parts of his body. He doesn't seem to be able to teleport larger weapons (such as tanks) but it may be he simply isn't trying. His equipment includes a jet pack, but he doesn't routinely carry it. Any equipment that is destroyed is replaced if Landmines teleports home. He has a vast castle bristling with weaponry in whatever strange dimension the Gods call home. He is, of course, rich beyond all dreams of avarice.

Weapons: A hand that explodes as a grenade (5 dice, Radius 5/10/15 ft, Success 4+/5+/6). A mini gun (+3), also replacing his right hand—Landmines must teleport or change form (see below) to get it. A VERY big sword (+2)—extrudes from his left hand. A .44 magnum revolver. A bandoleer of grenades (as above), throwing knives, and ammunition. Camouflaged Kevlar body armour which changes coloration and pattern to match his surroundings, absorbs two hits. His left eye is a camera with light amplification, zoom lens and thermal imaging capabilities. He appears to be able to hear and transmit radio signals, and can communicate with cell-phones.

Notes: Landmines' Mystic Power is used to teleport (one round of concentration is needed, so the talent is rarely useful in combat), as a defence against the Mystic Powers of others, as a direct attack—a bolt of lightning from his hand—and to overcome the will of the feeble-minded (e.g. Extras); he can't use it on anyone with Thinking (2) or better, and it can be resisted by the Mystic Power of victims. Finally, he can use the power to assume the form of anyone of approximately his size and build. While disguised he cannot use his other attacks or powers; it takes him a round (during which he cannot fight) to change form.

If Landmines is killed his body self-destructs but a new one is built by his supernatural servants; it takes several weeks. He generally comes back with new gadgetry implanted.

Queen Elizabeth (AKA "The Queenmother")

Status: 50 (Villain)
Success: 4+
Armour: -2
Hit Points: 10
Bonus Points:
Attributes:
  Animal Handler (2)
  Athlete (4)
  Charisma (5)
  Driving (3)
  Luck (2)
  Marksmanship (6)
  Martial Arts (6)
  Mystic Power (6)
  Speed (4)
  Strength (5)
  Thief (3)
  Thinking (4)

Quote: "Now my plot has Diana in its coils, and soon she will pay the price of her disobedience. Nyah-ha-ha-ha-ha!"

Back Story: Queen Elizabeth rules England; she is secretly the criminal genius known as the Queenmother, involved in international arms and tobacco trading. She wears a crown, long white gloves, and an ermine robe over armour.

Her crown and mace are both add +2 to her Mystic Power; the crown gives her mind control powers, used mainly to "manage" her son and husband (who is rarely seen and appears to be in the last stages of senility), and to punish underlings who fail her. It uses her boosted Mystic Power to attack the victim's Mystic Power plus Thinking. Her mace can project a stream of energy which inflicts pain and injury while simultaneously rejuvenating the Queen. Her ungloved touch can cause diseases which can only be cured by Mystic Power. Without the regalia she still has these powers, but gains no bonuses. The regalia can be used to boost anyone's Mystic Powers, even Diana, but they tend to exert an unwholesome influence on their user.

It is obvious that she has been seduced by the Dark Side of the Mystic Powers of Royalty. She is an ally of Landmines, but intolerant of his "weakness" towards Diana. Eventually she plans to depose him and take his place as God of War. She or her underlings are likely to appear in any adventure set in England.

Elizabeth will always leave her victims alive and suffering, or in elaborate death traps, in preference to killing them quickly.

Possessions: Castle, various cars and yachts, and anything else money can buy. Since she effectively owns England she can take anything that isn't for sale.

Weapons: Crown (see above) and Mace. The ray projected by the Mace drains hit points; the effect reverses if the attack is interrupted before Elizabeth is ready. It can be resisted by Mystic Power and deflected by mirrors. For every 5 hits the ray drains, Elizabeth gains +1 Status. The mace can also be used as an ordinary Martial Arts weapon (+1). She also carries two katanas (+2) which she can use for two simultaneous Martial Arts attacks, and often has a pump shotgun (+2) handy.

Notes: Fighting Elizabeth hand to hand is usually a very bad idea, but adventurers will have to get past her large and well-equipped household guard to do so anyway. Her palace is full of death traps, escape chutes, hidden panels, and concealed weapons. She has returned from apparent death on several occasions, usually finding Charlie attempting to rule England in her place. The Regalia has also survived destruction at least once.

Thatcher The Sorceress
(Undead Chancellor of Evil)

Status: 40 (Villain)
Success: 5+
Hit Points: 8
Bonus Points:
Attributes:
Charisma (4)
Computers (1)
Marksmanship (5)
Martial Arts (6)
Mystic Power (9)
Speed (6)
Strength (4)
Thief (2)
Thinking (3)

Quote: "You can't pay? There really is no alternative. Guards, take him away..."

Back Story: Thatcher is Queen Elizabeth's chancellor and adviser, and is plotting to seize her throne. She has several duties, the most important of them is to squeeze taxes from London, which she does with ruthless efficiency. She is also a powerful wizard who has transcended death itself.

In London most public areas have a gigantic poster of Thatcher, usually guarded by uniformed thugs. The eyes occasionally glow red and follow the movements of passers-by. If Thatcher makes an announcement (usually of a new tax) the posters animate. Sometimes graffiti artists try to deface the posters; they typically suffer unlikely accidents (think of The Omen) within moments. There are also giant statues of Thatcher that animate (use the stats for golems above, but add more hit points) if she wills it. The largest is on top of the column in Trafalgar Square. She is supernaturally beautiful, a magical illusion. She employs hordes of tax collectors in a variety of guises; 'Traffic Wardens', 'Inland Revenue', and the dreaded 'Poll Tax Collectors' and 'VAT Inspectors'. Like Queen Elizabeth, she has apparently been killed but returned on several occasions. She often appears if an episode is set in London.

Thatcher will always leave her victims alive and suffering, or in elaborate death traps, in preference to killing them quickly.

Possessions: She appears to need no possessions other than ordinary clothing and a monk-like hooded cape (used to shield her from sunlight if she has to travel by day, see below). She is rumoured to occasionally sleep in a coffin by day, but nobody knows where it is or what would happen if it were destroyed, and in any case she rarely sleeps.

Weapons: Thatcher relies mainly on her guards, resorting to personal combat as a last resort. If necessary she will use telekinesis to seize weapons and her speed to duck away from bullets, martial artists, and other problems.

Notes: Thatcher is undead; she cannot stand the touch of sunlight, and loses 1 hit point for every round she is exposed to it (every three rounds if cloaked). Her Mystic Powers let her disguise herself and underlings as other people or inanimate objects (an attack against the Thinking or Mystic Power attribute, whichever is stronger, of those she is trying to deceive). She can also reduce the level of light in any enclosed space (such as a room); if she achieves four or more successes all light (other than natural sunlight) is blanked out. She can use telekinesis on inanimate objects up to the size of a small car, wielding them as weapons with her Martial Arts or Marksmanship attributes. She can also levitate (but can't do both simultaneously). Her most impressive power is the ability to see through the eyes of her posters and statues anywhere in London, and to project her telekinesis and illusions through these images.

Archer The Assassin

Status: 25 (Henchman)
Success: 5
Hit Points: 5
Bonus Points:
  Athlete (4)
  Driving (3)
  Marksmanship (5)
  Martial Arts (2)
  Science (2)
  Speed (3)
  Strength (2)
  Thief (2)
  Thinking (2)

Quote: (in a hoarse whisper) "The Lady Thatcher sends her greetingssss..."

Back Story: Archer is Thatcher's right-hand man(?). He is never seen, except as a cloaked and hooded figure with gloved hands, and there are hints that he may be the evil twin of one of the major series characters; probably Red Ken or Fergie, possibly Diana herself. It isn't certain that Archer is male or even human. He seems to be seriously unlucky, since his attempts to assassinate Red Ken and Diana have consistently failed, or may be playing a deeper game and missing intentionally. He only appears as Thatcher's accomplice, never on his own. The referee should decide the truth about this enigmatic figure.

Possessions: Cell-phone, innocent-looking cosmetics concealing poisons and the components of his weapons.

Weapons: Archer chooses his weapons to fit his plans, but is most typically armed with a crossbow with poisoned bolts (+1 dice, 4 dice poison attack). He has also used rifles (+1 or +2 depending on the model used), throwing knives and stars, sword sticks, lasers, and poisons. He tries to avoid hand-to-hand combat, preferring to strike from a distance or by stealth.

Notes: Archer's real goals are enigmatic; he appears to be loyal to Thatcher, but if so he is an underachiever. Despite the fact that he has failed her on several occasions she has not killed him, which also seems odd. The referee should decide what's really going on.

Queen Victoria

Status: 30 (guest star)
Success: 5+
Armour: See Below
Hit Points: 6
Bonus Points:
Attributes:
  Animal Handler (3)
  Charisma (4)
  Computers (5)
  Luck (4)
  Marksmanship (2)
  Martial Arts (1)
  Mystic Power (6)
  Thinking (5)

Quote: "You wish our armies to withdraw? We are not amused..."

Back Story: Queen Victoria rules Britannia, England's neighbouring kingdom, whose capital is the city of Windsor. She is the benevolent middle-aged monarch of a rapidly expanding empire spread by her fierce red-coated beefeater soldiers. She argues that the countries they conquer are happier under her rule, which may be true but doesn't convince states bordering her empire. Britannia has many claims to fame, not least the Bomb developed by Victoria's husband, Prince Albert Einstein.

Victoria has mixed feelings about Diana; she likes her and appreciates her good intentions, but isn't prepared to let her jeopardise the security of Britannia or the expansion of the Empire. Sometimes Diana thwarts her plans; within days Victoria, a military genius, comes up with new strategies. Nevertheless Diana and Fergie are welcome at her palace, since Diana has twice helped to save Victoria from Elizabeth's assassins. Naturally various map rooms and command bunkers are kept firmly locked when they are around.

Victoria does not believe in Landmines, but several of her Generals are dedicated to his service. If Diana can prove he exists Victoria may turn to the cause of peace.

Possessions: She lives quietly, but in modest luxury, rarely travelling far from home although she undoubtedly owns aircraft, cars, and other vehicles. Her war room has complex punched-card computers, map tables, and communications

facilities.

Weapons: Victoria is never armed, but always escorted by a few beefeaters and her fierce woad-daubed Scots bodyguard John Brown, a legendary barbarian warrior:

Typical Beefeater *Attack:* Martial Arts (3), Marksmanship (4), *Success:* 6 Hits: 2 *Notes:* Strength (2), Rifle +1

John Brown *Attack:* Martial Arts (5), Marksmanship (6), *Success:* 6 Hits: 3 *Notes:* Strength (2), Speed (2), Machine gun +2, axes +1, grenades, Sword +2

Notes: Victoria's Mystic Powers of Royalty include a force screen which counters damage and has saved her from several assassination attempts (subtract the number of successes she makes from the number of hits that try to penetrate), a healing touch, and the ability to somehow enforce the oath sworn by Beefeaters, who will never betray her; when Elizabeth infiltrated agents into Victoria's bodyguard they switched allegiance on taking the oath, and are now fanatically loyal servants of Victoria. This last power pits her Mystic Power against the Beefeater's Thinking plus Mystic Power attributes; if they are overcome the Beefeater will always be loyal, regardless of earlier intentions.

Prince Albert Einstein

Status: 20 (Guest Star)
Success: 5+
Armour: (See Below)
Hit Points: 4
Bonus Points:
Attributes:
   Charisma (3)
   Computers (5)
   Marksmanship (1)
   Mystic Power (4)
   Thinking (7)
   Quote: "Ach so... Oh well, back to the drawing board..."
   Back Story:

Prince Albert Einstein is Victoria's consort, a German prince and scientist who spends most of his time in a laboratory. His inventions include The Bomb (never described more clearly), land leviathans, flying dreadnoughts, cruise missiles, and other weapons to make warfare "too horrible to contemplate". Most of the world's warlords happily contemplate such horror, and several now use his inventions, so he has begun trying to persuade Victoria to set an example by endorsing Diana's cause. He won't help Diana disrupt Victoria's plans, but won't do anything to stop her.

There have been attempts to kidnap Albert and steal the plans of The Bomb. Oddly Queen Elizabeth doesn't appear to be after it, implying that she may have it or something worse. Albert is likely to appear in any story involving Victoria, if only in the background.

Possessions: Numerous pocket tools, magnifiers, instruments, and gizmos.

Weapons: None carried, but he could probably improvise something in minutes in the laboratory, in an hour or two in a prison cell.

Notes: Albert's Mystic Powers of Royalty manifests as protection from injury; subtract the number of successes he makes from the number of hits if he is attacked or accidentally blows himself up. This is very useful in the laboratory... This is also one of Victoria's abilities, and it seems likely that he has "acquired" it from her.

Emperor Norton

Status: 25
 (Guest star)
Success: 5+
Hit Points: 5
Bonus Points: 10
Attributes:
 Artist (2)
 Charisma (6)
 Luck (4)
 Mystic Power (4)
 Science (4)
 Speed (5)
 Thief (5)
 Thinking (4)

Quote: "You will observe that there is nothing up my sleeve..."

Back Story: Emperor Norton is the benign ruler of large parts of America. He has the Mystic Powers of Royalty, but is more notable for luck and persuasiveness verging on hypnotism, and amazingly fast sleight of hand (via the Speed and Thief attributes). He can produce anything from a rabbit to a bazooka from his top hat, and often does so. He always seems to be able to produce small items such as a gun or lockpicks from nowhere, even if he has been repeatedly searched.

Norton is a fat jolly bearded man who wears a top hat and frock coat and smokes a corncob pipe. He is interested in space travel and is the founder of NASA (Norton's Agency for Space Achievement), which is preparing for the first expedition to the Moon.

Norton is secretly an alchemist, and in laboratories under his palace at Fort Knox has rediscovered the Philosopher's Stone, as well as building a golem, which is used to stir the cauldron in which the gold is made. Norton intends to use the gold to buy weapons and turn them into more gold, until there are no more weapons in the world.

Possessions: Norton always carries a large bag of gold, a few packs of cards, and other conjuring paraphernalia. He has vast stocks of gold at Fort Knox.

Weapons: Norton is a pacifist and never armed, but isn't an idiot and will help someone fight on his behalf if there is no alternative, if necessary by producing a weapon from nowhere. He is usually guarded by the Secret Service (all of whose agents wear jackets with the Secret Service logo, an eye in a pyramid):

Secret Service Agent *Attack:* Martial Arts (5), Marksmanship (6) *Success:* 6 *Hits:* 3 *Notes:* Strength (1), Speed (3), Automatic +1 or Machine Pistol +1, headset radio.

Notes: Norton's Mystic Power can be added to his Speed, Thief, Luck, or Charisma attributes at will. It can also be used (with at least TWO successes) to pull something out of thin air—he has no idea how he does it, or where the things he produces come from, but teleportation seems the most likely explanation.

Diana Does Dallas
A DIANA: WARRIOR PRINCESS Adventure
For 2-6 Players.

It is assumed that the players are taking the roles of Diana and Fergie, and optionally Red Ken or other guest stars. A subplot involving Wild Bill Gates, Bonnie Prince Charlie, and Ron L. Hubble is described below; for different characters some other plot may be needed. The entire adventure should take no more than 2-3 hours to play as written; however, referees should feel free to add complications and additional scenes and subplots as may seem appropriate.

The adventure begins *in media res*, in the middle of action—don't worry how the stars got into this situation, it really isn't at all relevant to the plot! If more than three characters are in use the others should enter the story later.

Teaser

A strange temple (curiously similar to St. Paul's Cathedral, but with a glass dome) on a deserted moor. Rain, thunder, and lightning outside. Inside, Fergie is hunging upside-down from a rope tied around her ankles, over a pit full of smouldering tobacco, with a candle slowly burning through the rope, watched by hordes of cigarette-smoking near-zombie worshippers chanting and coughing in unison. Overhead are dozens of huge banners, each bearing a different cigarette logo. As the action begins Diana and Red Ken plummet through the dome, absailing down ropes towards the crowd below. Broken glass showers down, fortunately hitting nobody important, and Diana shouts "Fergie—don't inhale!"

A fight with about ten or twelve worshippers per character should be a brisk workout for the adventurers; they can be demoralised by a spectacular attack, and the diversion gives Fergie a chance to swing clear, grab a cultist and drop him into the pit, swing on the banners, or find some other way to escape. It's likely that Diana or Ken will swing to free her, but she has at least a round to get free on her own. Fergie still has two concealed knives, which the cultists somehow missed, and can use them to fight, get free, or both. If the fight seems to be going really badly the worshippers start to collapse, coughing and choking, as the lethal tobacco catches up with them.

As the last worshippers go down (or earlier if it seems dramatically appropriate) the High Priest appears, wielding a magical staff shaped like a giant cigarette in a holder; he'll attack whoever seems to be most dangerous. He's backed up by three priests with machine pistols and nunchuks. All wear robes cut to resemble the cigarette packet of your choice. Be prepared to change this scene if the adventurers don't co-operate; for example, if they decide to rescue Fergie and climb back up the ropes, the High Priest, priests, and some cultists can be waiting for them on the roof. Whatever happens, the rope shouldn't finish burning until Fergie has just been pulled to safety (or somehow saves herself).

Worshippers *Attack:* Martial Arts (1) *Success:* 6 *Hits:* 1 *Notes:* Club, no bonus

Priests *Attack:* Martial Arts (2), Marksmanship (3) *Success:* 6 *Hits:* 2 *Notes:* Machine Pistol +1, Nunchuks +1

High Priest *Attack:* Martial Arts (4), Marksmanship (5) *Success:* 5+ *Hits:* 5 *Notes:* Mystic Power (3), Cigarette Staff +1 (see below).

The Staff can be used like a gun (firing a jet of smoke) or as a quarter-staff. Each time the High Priest succeeds in hitting someone roll his Mystic Power. The victim goes into a coughing fit lasting one round for each success; this attack can be resisted by Strength or Mystic Power. The staff can take 4 hits before shattering.

If the High Priest's staff is smashed, it is engulfed in flickering green flames then disintegrates and the temple starts to collapse. If the adventurers don't smash the staff deliberately, it shatters as the priest goes down. Tiles, pieces of glass, and stones start to fall from the roof, fotunately without hitting anyone important. There's just time to sprint or climb to safety before the temple implodes completely.

As the adventurers get their breath back Diana's cell-phone beeps, and sticks out a tongue of ticker-tape, a text message:

DIANA, URGENTLY NEED YOUR HELP IN DALLAS, SOME BASTARD IS TRYING TO KILL KENNY. NORTON.

Cue music, and cue titles.

Referee's Information

Diana, Fergie, and Red Ken all owe Emperor Norton debts of gratitude; he has aided them many times in the past, and his vast fortune helps finance the underground resistance to the evil Queen Elizabeth and her chancellor Thatcher. If run as player characters they shouldn't hesitate to help him. If Red Ken is an NPC he can't leave for the moment; the London Underground has first call on his time, and there will be an important meeting in a few days. He whistles for his horse, apologises, and rides off into the sunset towards London.

While Emperor Norton rules much of America, he is a benign monarch who leaves the day-to-day running of his empire to elected officials such as President John F. Kenny. Unfortunately Kenny has been targeted by Landmines, who sees an opportunity to stir up trouble. The instrument of his plot is Elliot Ness, leader of the Untouchables (a caste of sanitation workers, cleaners, maids, and other "mucky" trades shunned by the rest of society, whose members are given sole responsibility for cleaning up America).

Currently Kenny and Ness are negotiating an end to this segregation, civil reforms that will allow the Untouchables to change jobs and marry outside their caste. Ness claims to want this done immediately, while Kenny has proposed a series of gradual changes that will give America time to get used to the idea. Apparently they are in broad agreement but disagree on the time scale for the change. In fact while most Untouchables want an end to this discrimination, Ness earns vast amounts of money by acting as middle-man between them and their employers, and would be ruined if they were free to mingle with the rest of society. Landmines has "persuaded" him that the way to resolve the problem is to have Kenny assassinated by Untouchable extremists; with Kenny dead the negotiations will collapse, and probably many years will pass before they resume.

For secrecy the negotiations are being held aboard the riverboat *Norman Bates*, currently moored in Dallas Harbour but about to cruise down-river to Boston.

Four days ago a maid put a small bomb in Kenny's suite before he arrived; it exploded as she armed it—Landmines supplied the bomb, which was unnecessarily difficult to arm safely—and killed her without harming anyone else. Currently the Secret Service assumes that she found and accidentally triggered the bomb while cleaning the room.

Two days ago a cleaner dropped burning rags down a ventilation funnel leading to Kenny's cabin. Fortunately the Secret Service agents soon stamped it out; the observation deck where the rags were dropped was open to the public, but only someone intimate with the layout of the boat would know where the funnel led, let alone who occupied the cabin.

Ness has told some of the more militant Untouchables that Kenny is refusing to budge on the timing, and warned them "not to do anything rash", stirring things more as seems appropriate. This led to the first two assassination attempts, and will lead to more. If all else fails Ness has a team of mercenaries standing by, plus three steam-powered helicopter gunships "borrowed" from the Dallas Sanitation Department (don't ask why the Dallas Sanitation Department needs helicopter gunships, you probably won't like the answer). Landmines has taken control of the pilots and is already planning to use these craft for his own amusement.

The adventure should consist of:

☀The teaser.

✵A meeting with Norton.

♟An interlude aboard the boat (possibly involving the sub-plot below) in which the adventurers save Kenny from two more assassination attempts, and possibly try to help Kenny and Ness with the negotiations.

🜛A helicopter attack on the boat, ending with the boat sinking and the adventurers, Ness, and Kenny in life rafts and separated from other survivors.

❂An alligator attack on the rafts, and discovery that the rafts are heading for rapids.

❂A trek across the desert.

🥃An encounter with hostile Indians.

☙The arrival of Ness's mercenaries, and a big fight scene.

⌗Revelation of Ness's guilt and Landmines' involvement.

∾Fade-out to (hopefully) happy ending.

The plot is linear, but referees should be prepared to improvise extra encounters and scenes as they become necessary, especially for larger groups of players. Some examples are briefly described below.

Sub-Plot: A Cure For Lepus

This optional section is an example of how to keep some players busy when a large group of characters would be awkward. The early stages of the main plot work reasonably well for a group of two to four players; more tend to get in each other's way. Later stages (after the *Norman Bates* sinks) are suitable for up to six characters. This sub-plot can be used to keep Gates, Hubble and Charlie busy if present. Some background is mentioned on the record sheets for Hubble and Charlie; if you use this plot brief the players involved separately from the rest.

A few days ago, in New York, Hubble sold Charlie a thousand shares in RLH Pharmaceuticals, a fake company which claims to be on the verge of a cure for Lepus[10] (which hitherto has only been curable by the Mystic Powers of Royalty). He wants to sell Charlie another 20,000 shares but first Charlie must be convinced that the cure works. Once Hubble learned that Diana was on the way to Dallas (he doesn't know that Kenny or Ness is present, he just heard that Diana was arriving) he arranged to meet Charlie in Dallas for a demonstration. He has also found a Lepus patient, Miss Charlotte Bronte (a Speaking Extra with Charisma (2) but no other relevant attributes), and persuaded her to go along with the scam.

Hubble showed Charlotte to Charlie and pretended to inoculate her with the Lepus vaccine, saying that it would take forty-eight hours to work. Charlotte will intercept Diana and ask for a cure. Once she is cured he plans to show her to Charlie again, but needless to say the story will fall apart if Charlie knows that Diana cured Charlotte; Hubble needs to keep him busy and out of the way somehow. Gambling aboard the *Norman Bates* seems like a good idea; he isn't aware that Diana or Wild Bill will be aboard. Needless to say, if Charlie sees Diana he may learn that she might have cured Charlotte, and the scam will fall apart.

Charlie only knows that Hubble has sold him some shares and wants to sell him more. Hubble has promised to show him the effect of the new anti-Lepus vaccine within a few hours, and meanwhile has given him some gambling chips and a tall drink to keep him amused.

Gates knows none of this, and has no idea Diana will aboard;

---

10. Yes, Lepus still means "rabbits".

he knows that part of one deck has been closed off, but has no idea why. However, that all fades into insignificance next to the arrival of Charlie, the world's worst gambler, and Hubble, his old foe. Fleecing them ought to be a lot of fun.

Keep the three working (and playing) at cross purposes until the boat is attacked, then they should join the other adventurers for the final scenes.

The NORMAN BATES

The next scene begins with the adventurers' flying boat touching down in Dallas harbour (oddly, a coastal harbour which looks strangely like Sydney) and taxi-ing to a landing stage.

A Cure For Lepus: If you are using this sub-plot a young woman covered in horrible supperating boils, the unmistakable symptom of Lepus, runs up to Diana as she steps ashore and asks her to lay on her hands and cure her. This is an easy use of Diana's Mystic Power, requiring only one success; if she fails on her first attempt she can try again (two successes needed) and even a third time (three successes needed). If all attempts fail Charlotte will not be cured, otherwise the boils start to vanish. It's an everyday event for Diana, and she should shake off the grateful Charlotte without realising that the meeting has been carefully contrived.

The adventurers are taken in a high speed motorcade to Norton's Dallas palace (which bears an uncanny resemblance to Sydney opera house from the outside, but looks like a Victorian mansion on the inside). Norton briefs the adventurers quickly, explaining about the negotiations and the assassination attempts. He can't do much more to help Kenny, who has a secret service guard, since it's his policy to avoid unnecessary intervention in civil affairs. "Unofficial" protection from Diana may be the best way to keep Kenny safe.

Norton suspects that the assassins may be agents of Queen Elizabeth. He has no evidence for this, but his Secret Service has recently uncovered one of Elizabeth's criminal syndicates, so the assassination attempts may be her revenge. It's a complete red herring, but in the absence of real information it's as good a theory as any. If anyone suggests that Diana might do better to investigate this theory Norton explains that some of his best agents are on the crime case already, working under cover. They've found no signs of an assassination plot; the agents are still on the case, and might be endangered if Diana gets involved.

Before they leave Norton gives Diana and her companions passes that will identify them to his Secret Service agents aboard the boat; without them they won't be allowed anywhere near Kenny.

The *Norman Bates* is a huge five-decked luxury paddle-steamer with three saloons, a restaurant, a casino, and hotel accommodation. Below decks are the crew accommodation, reactor, boilers, and other machinery, on the first and second decks are the casino and other public facilities, on the third to fifth decks are hotel-style accommodation. Precise game data for the boat isn't given because it is destined to be sunk on cue.

The boat doesn't have facilities for any vehicles or horses that might have accompanied the adventurers, even Diana will be asked to leave her motorcycle behind. Emperor Norton will arrange to have it transported to Boston by air.

The precise layout of the boat isn't actually very important. Keep things vague as characters move around. Don't worry about money when characters go shopping; assume that everyone has enough for their immediate needs, but not so much that they can buy everything in a shop, or break the bank at the casino.

The area below decks is dominated by the huge nuclear reactors (which for some odd reasons have stokers who load in shovels of "fuel pellets"), boilers, and the rest of the engine machinery. Huge steel pistons slide back and forward in compartments under the floor, covered by steel gratings, making a horrible grinding noise. Two holds contain crates, furniture, sacks, barrels, and other cargo.

This area also has cabins for the working crew (not the officers) and a dormitory for the boat's Untouchables; while the crew have reasonably comfortable cabins with a degree of sound-proofing, the Untouchables have hammocks and their quarters have rusty steel walls with no sound-proofing whatever. This should be proof, if there was any doubt, of their unfair treatment.

The shops, bars and restaurants are tourist traps, expensive and indifferent quality.

The gun shop on Deck 2 is most likely to attract interest; Red Ken can replenish his stocks of throwing stars and knives, Fergie can get knives, Diana arrows, and anyone with a gun can buy ammunition; anything bought to replenish the character's existing arsenal will be of acceptably quality. Any new equipment (such as a high-powered rifle that isn't already recorded on the character's record) will be poorly made junk giving no bonus to marksmanship, and obviously unworthy of a true warrior's time or money. However, the equipment on sale includes six shoulder-fired missile launchers, with no bonus to marksmanship but explosive damage if they hit:

Small Missile *Dice:* 5 *Radius:* 5/10/15 ft *Success:* 4+/5+/6

They may come in useful later in the scenario, but they (and any other extra equipment the adventurers pick up) should be lost when the boat sinks.

Adventurers may think of buying maps in the book shop or gift shop; if so, give them a meaningless map consisting of a long squiggly line representing the river, with Dallas at one end and Boston at the other and numerous tributaries branching off or joining the river. It doesn't actually tell them much that's useful, or provide details such as a scale, but it's all that they are going to get.

Although part of one deck is closed off for the meeting, there are many other guests aboard, and the facilities offered include a fashionable casino. If Wild Bill Gates is appearing there "happens" to be a big-stakes poker game planned in the casino, while Ron L. Hubble might there pursuing a rich mark such as Bonnie Prince Charlie. If only one of these characters is involved find a way to involve him in the main plot; for example, he might accidentally spot the assassin in the third attempt below, before anyone else, and sound the alarm. If more than one of these characters is involved use the separate sub-plot involving all three, described above. The casino itself is simply a large compartment on deck 1 overlooked by a railed gallery on deck 2. There are gambling tables on both decks, the lower deck has a bar and the upper gallery a jazz band. There is always a crowd in the casino regardless of the time.

A Cure For Lepus: If you are using this sub-plot an encounter between Bonnie Prince Charlie and Diana might wreck Hubble's plans, so he should be given a chance to head off the adventurers whenever they seem likely to encounter him. Each attempt should be a closer shave than the last, and of course the presence of Diana aboard will soon be the subject of intense gossip and speculation. Bates shouldn't be prevented from meeting her, unless Hubble tries to stop that too—how Hubble will stop him from spilling the beans, especially if he is being run by a player, is left to the ingenuity of the players and/or referee.

In fact Charlie will not immediately realise the truth if they meet, even if the player running him makes the connection; he should make a Thinking roll, +1 for every time they meet and anything that is said to give Charlie more clues, if he ever succeeds he will know the truth. Needless to say the trick will be revealed if Diana encounters Charlotte Bronte while Charlie is around and says anything to reveal the truth. Hubble should think of warning Charlotte to keep out of sight, and will do so if he is being run as an NPC. Players should be left to think of this sort of things for themselves—Charlotte wants to have fun after years of disfiguring disease, and if she isn't warned off she'll be in the casino most of the evening.

Meeting Kenny

Ness and Kenny currently occupy two suites at the forward end of the fourth deck, meeting in a third. Two more suites are occupied by Secret Service guards, one is reserved for Diana and friends (with another marked "unused" available if needed), and one is used for a temporary galley serving these suites. Each suite has three bedrooms, a comfortable lounge, and a luxurious bathroom with jacuzzi. The forward half of the deck is closed off to everyone else; the forward stairs are closed by steel gates on the decks above and below (a nuisance to guests staying on deck 5), and there are guards to keep out the inquisitive. These guards are Secret Service agents (wearing blazers with discreet "eye in the Pyramid" badges, plus conspicuous earphones and microphones for their concealed radios—think 1940s telephone operator), led by an Agent Jackson. In all twenty Secret Service agents are assigned to the boat, working in shifts.

Secret Service Agents *Attack:* Martial Arts (2), Marksmanship (2) *Success:* 6 *Hits:* 1 *Notes:* Strength (1), Pistol, radio, dark glasses.

Agent Jackson *Attack:* Martial Arts (3), Marksmanship (4), *Success:* 6 *Hits:* 3 *Notes:* Strength (2), Speed (3), Machine pistol +1, radio, dark glasses.

Once the adventurers are identified they'll be allowed to see President Kenny—if they try to get to him without identifying themselves the Secret Service agents will fight to the death.

President Kenny

Status: 20
(Guest Star)
Success: 5+
Hit Points: 4
Bonus Points:
Attributes:
Animal
handling (2)
Artist
(musician) (2)
Charisma (4)
Computers (1)
Luck (2)
Marksmanship (2)
Martial Arts (1)
Science (1)
Speed (2)
Thinking (3)

Kenny is a short middle-aged man, and when first encountered has severe laryngitis (the result of hours of negotiations over several days) and can't talk above a whisper; he wears a hooded bath-robe and spends most of his time hunched over a bowl of steaming water trying to get his voice back. To the adventurers his voice sounds like an incomprehensible muffled whisper, but his secretary, Mrs. Altavista, effortlessly translates. He recovers overnight without help, or can be cured in an hour or so with some of the herbs from Fergie's first aid kit and an easy Healing roll. Diana's Mystic Powers won't work, they aren't effective against laryngitis.

Kenny is a charismatic politician and loyal servant of Emperor Norton. Outside politics he is a VERY boring man, although like most rich Americans he owns a ranch and will always be interested in talking about horses, coypu and other farm stock.

Via his secretary Kenny explains that the negotiations are currently deadlocked; Ness wants to tear down the entire caste system immediately, Kenny favours a more gradual approach which will phase in changes over five years. If asked why, he explains that while he has every sympathy for the Untouchables, the main reason is economic; every cleaning contract in America would have to be bid on or re-negotiated at phenomenal cost. If the changes are phased in gradually most contracts will run out naturally, and there might even be some small savings. This last is a clue, although Kenny doesn't think to stress it; the Untouchables have a total lock on the cleaning business, and Ness and his staff negotiate most contracts. Ness takes a hidden cut of these transactions, and has a sizeable fortune in various foreign banks. He will lose this income if the Untouchables no longer have a monopoly, and would like to extend the time offered by Kenny to at least ten years. Unfortunately most Untouchables have other ideas, and he is under growing pressure to force Kenny to change the law.

During the first meeting with Kenny there is another assassination attempt; a sniper attack from a building near the harbour (yes, it's a book depository).

Give Diana and Fergie (and Ken if present) a chance to see the sniper before the shot is fired; if they know it's coming either Diana or Fergie can deflect the bullet with her sword (two successes needed; Speed plus Martial Arts can be used) or even bat it back towards the assassin (three successes needed to hit). If either deflects the bullet without saying where she wants it to go it ricochets in the cabin; this gives the other a chance to deflect it into a chair, or some other harmless target.

Ken can't deflect bullets since he doesn't have a sword, but can attempt to catch them in flight without injury; this needs Speed and Martial Arts for three successes, any failure means he will be shot by the assassin; Marksmanship (3), Martial Arts (2), success 6, +1 rifle, 3 hits.

If all else fails Agent Jackson leaps in front of President Kenny and is shot.

If Diana and co. drop everything else they can try to capture the assassin, otherwise the Secret Service will do so. He is dressed as an Untouchable sanitation worker and had his rifle concealed in a sack of litter. He has no identification or records. Naturally he will refuse to talk, and there is no immediate proof of any larger conspiracy. Before he can be properly interrogated there will be a powerful explosion in his cell, which kills him and two guards. Nobody can guess how he got the bomb (Landmines gave him a hand; if the bomb fragments are examined closely pieces of curved metal resembling fingers will be found) but now the Secret Service suspects a conspiracy and won't let Untouchables such as the maids near Kenny's cabin unless the adventurers intervene. Needless to say this will not help the negotiations!

A more thorough investigation will eventually identify the assassin as Achmed Cohen, a Chinese mercenary who has turned up in various combat zones over the last five or ten years. He's regarded as extremely dangerous. Nobody knows why he should be in Dallas, he wasn't even known to be in America.

The adventurers will probably want to talk to Ness at some point; he hasn't been targeted by the assassins so they may suspect him, but there isn't much real evidence. Naturally Ness will play the injured innocent (especially if Untouchables are being stopped too openly), denounce Kenny's laryngitis as a "typical sleazy trick to delay negotiations", insist that "My fellow Untouchables want this iniquity to end now, not in five or ten years.", and aim to get the adventurers to believe that he is the injured party.

Elliot Ness

Status: 20
  (Guest Star)
Success: 5+
Hit Points: 4
Bonus Points:
Attributes:
  Athlete (2)
  Charisma (3)
  Driving (2)
  Marksmanship (4)
  Martial Arts (3)
  Speed (1)
  Strength (1)
  Thinking (4)

A tall handsome man who by habit avoids touching anyone outside his caste; he will be extraordinarily surprised and embarassed if anyone insists on shaking hands or

touches him. He has an insincere moist handshake. He has a very small radio transmitter (not a cellphone) concealed in a yellow plastic action figure representing the ancient poet Homer, and will use it if he wants to summon his mercenaries. Note that even if he is searched this should be treated as a normal possession, since small religious fetishes of this type are very common.

Ness has a staff of two Untouchable sectretaries, both ignorant of his real motives, and an Untouchable bodyguard named Frank Nitti. Nitti is aware of Ness's activities but completely loyal, and is Ness's liason with the more militant Untouchables. Unfortunately he doesn't have full control over them and isn't aware of Landmines' involvement in their plans.

Frank Nitti *Status:* 10 (Extra) *Success:* 6 *Hits:* 2
Attributes: Driving (3), Marksmanship (2), Martial Arts (3), Speed (2), Pistol +2, Brass knuckles +1).

Down The River

The *Norman Bates* is due to sail on the evening following the unsuccessful assassination, and will do so unless the adventurers do something to intervene. Agent Jackson will oppose a change in plans, since it will be easier to maintain security once they are clear of the harbour and other boats. As it chugs from the harbour the city lights vanish from view surprisingly quickly, and a light mist gradually conceals the river banks. A slow bell tolls from the bridge of the boat, warning other craft of its passage. Somewhere on deck a crewman plays the "Duelling Banjos" theme, quickly interrupted as an officer orders him to get some work done.

Nothing much should happen overnight; it's hot and humid, a steamy heat which saps the energy of even the strongest Warrior Princess. Clothing sticks damply to flesh and most adventurers will probably want to shower and get to bed, hoping that the weather will be better in the morning. However, the casino and bars have full air-conditioning, so any marathon poker games Gates or Hubble might be playing can continue into the early hours of the morning.

A Cure For Lepus: If Charlie is being run as an NPC he seems not to notice the time; he should be on a moderately good winning streak. This means that Hubble also needs to stay around and be ready to fend off Diana or anything else that might give his trick away. And with Charlie and Hubble around

Gates should feel compelled to stay in the casino, if only to find out what Hubble is up to...

If all three are run by player characters resolve the game by luck rolls, each roll representing an hour or so of play. Anyone winning in three successive hours cleans out the other two, anyone coming last in two successive rounds is broke, otherwise play continues.

If you run this right it can end with all three sitting at a poker table, still nominally playing the game, but in fact asleep until they are disturbed by cleaners in the morning.

Who falls asleep? This is basically a contest of Strength— have each player roll Strength at 2 a.m., then every hour after that. When someone fails he falls asleep; however, everyone else must also roll again, and if anyone fails they also fall asleep! Repeat unless nobody falls asleep; that yawning and snoring can be downright infectious...

If anyone sets out to search the boat, either during the night or the following morning, they should eventually stumble across another bomb. It's down in the engine room, near the bows, and is a crude steel box welded to one of the girders, fastened closed with a padlock (make a Thief roll to pick it with a hairpin, wire, or lockpicks). There is a loud ticking clock. In fact this bomb has been placed by Nitti, as a way of disrupting the talks and diverting attention from the Untouchables. There are two sticks of dynamite inside, which isn't enough to do more than make a loud bang and buckle the hull plates a little. Of course it will hurt anyone standing close if it explodes:

Dynamite *Dice:* 2 per stick *Radius:* 5/10/20 ft
Success: 4+/5+/6

The bomb explodes about half an hour after it is found if nothing is done. It can be defused by making an easy Science roll (provided an electrical tool kit is used—there are several aboard); if the roll fails it will not explode immediately, but will start to whir and click for a couple of rounds, time enough to get clear, before exploding. If any of the stars or co-stars are caught in the blast they should be lightly singed or injured but not killed, even if this means fudging the dice roll a little: "Fortunately the steel casing diverts some of the blast upwards, taking off—oh (roll dice while hiding it from the players)—two hits. You survive... just."

Naturally the Secret Service detail includes agents with bomb disposal skills; if one is let loose on the bomb he will defuse it easily.

Another way to handle this is to cut the box free of the hull and throw it into the river; it will explode seconds after it goes in, regardless of the time left, drenching all onlookers and throwing a large fish out of the water to hit Fergie if she is present.

Meanwhile the negotiations should be continuing, possibly interrupted by the Secret Service guards hustling Kenny to the other end of the boat while the bomb is defused, loud arguments about the precise timing of the change in the status of Untouchables, and gradual concessions by Kenny who is slowly pushed down from five to three years, to Ness's well-concealed dismay. Diana should take the credit for this if she takes part in the negotiations as a disinterested third party. Ness refuses to budge an inch on timing, repeating again and again that the Untouchables have already waited far too long. If anyone doubts his word he'll take them down to see the squalor of the Untouchable quarters below deck. If the boat hasn't previously been searched this is a good opportunity to find the bomb, which should be somewhere near their quarters instead of the bow.

A Cure For Lepus: It's time to wrap up this plot. During the afternoon, if Hubble's scam hasn't already been blown, he takes Charlotte to meet Charlie again, as proof that she has been permanently cured of Lepus. If Charlie still doesn't suspect he will probably decide to invest; just as he is about to hand over a bag of gold Diana or Fergie should wander by (this may need careful timing), recognise Charlotte, and say something to reveal the deception. If the players running Diana and/or Fergie don't seem to want to cooperate by saying something, have Charlie make an additional Thinking roll at +2 dice as he sees them. If that also fails, Charlotte breaks down as she sees Diana/Fergie and reveals how she was really cured. She sobs that she never wanted to defraud anyone, she just wanted to be cured, she didn't realise that Hubble was such a crook, and so forth. Hopefully this ends with Charlie about to thrash Hubble (unless he talks very fast) and Gates "comforting" the sobbing Charlotte. But the main plot is about to intervene...

As evening approaches everyone involved in the negotiations should feel that a good deal has been done, and will be reasonably happy that things are under control. It's time to hear the distant thunder of rotor blades...

Rum Tumpety Tum Tum, Tumpety Tum Tum...

Landmines is about to pull his big surprise. He has used his Mystic Power to subvert the crew of Ness's helicopters, and they are about to attack the boat. The aim of this scene is to sink the boat without seriously harming any of the adventurers, Ness, or Kenny; everyone else is expendable. At this point the boat is chugging along a broad river running through a deep ravine; if anyone asks, they're somewhere in Indian territory.

There are three steam-powered helicopters, all marked as belonging to the Dallas Sanitation Department.

Helicopter Pilots *Status:* 10 *Success:* 6 *Hits:* 2 *Attributes:* Drive (4), Marksmanship (4), Speed (2).

The helicopters are slightly different to the design in the main rules, mounting torpedoes rather than missiles and cellphone/radio jammers. These will block any transmissions from the boat throughout the attack.

Attack Helicopter *Speed:* 200 MPH *Armour:* -2 *Hits:* 10 *Weapons & Notes:* 2 Rotary cannon +4, 4 torpedoes (as missiles), Radio/cellphone jammer.

The helicopters take turns attacking the boat; it takes two rounds to line up to strafe the boat or drop a torpedo, then the helicopter is in range for another two rounds after the attack. If anyone has been shopping (or visited the gun shop) the missiles and other weapons on sale may be very useful. However, the helicopters are vulnerable to handguns, bows, and even thrown weapons such as shurikin or knives throughout the attack. As they sweep in the Secret Service agents hustle Kenny and Ness away from the windows, while tearing off their headsets because they are deafened by the radio jamming. All of the following were tried in play-tests:

❀Grabbing a spring-board from the gymnasium and using it to launch an athlete up to grab the skids of a helicopter and try to climb in to attack the pilot. This requires a difficult Athlete roll (which could be combined with Strength, Speed or Mystic Power), but will work if at least two successes are rolled. In the fight the pilot will lose control and spin into the river, the attacker will be thrown free with bruises and one or two hits lost.

❀Throwing a cloud of shurikin or knives at a helicopter, hoping to hit a steam line or some other vital component; this requires at least two successes, but since the helicopter is armoured -2 they're needed anyway. Any damage that gets through the armour should be taken from the helicopter's hits.

❀Targetting the pilot or one of the torpedoes (using a bow or gun, possibly aided by the Mystic Power of Royalty);

❀The windscreens of the helicopters are armoured -1 only (a serious design flaw) so it's easier to harm the pilot than the aircraft; however, if the pilot is killed he will try to crash into the boat as he dies, succeeding unless something else destroys the helicopter.

❀The detonators have no armour, but are very small targets and difficult to hit, but if they are hit the torpedo will explode and take out the helicopter. However, the pilot won't be killed instantly, and will ram the boat as it crashes.

❀Using Diana's Mystic Power of Royalty, Strength and Marksmanship to throw her sword at one of the helicopters as it flies past. It neatly cuts through the tail rotor before flying back to her hand, the helicopter spins out of control and crashes— into the boat...

Whatever happens, end this scene with the boat hit by at least one torpedo or a crashed helicopter, on fire and sinking fast. **Fade out...**

The Morning After...

Fade in... At dawn the following morning the player characters, Kenny, and Ness are drifting along the river (which is still flowing through a ravine, but is much faster and narrower) in an inflatable life-raft. Kenny says "I guess the other boats must have drifted away from us in the night. It's kind of odd, I wonder if we've strayed into another stream or something..." It's very hot, and there don't seem to be any plants visible on the edges of the ravine.

Anyone who was injured has recovered hit points overnight. Any cellphones or radios the adventurers were carrying are useless, soaked in the wreck; if anyone tries to use one it short-circuits and burns, even after it has been dried out. Ness still has his concealed radio, but won't say so. A quick check of the boat reveals that there are no oars and few supplies aboard; nothing but the adventurers' personal possessions and weapons (less anything the referee wanted them to lose), a few cans with the labels soaked off (all contain beans in tomato sauce), two 5-litre water bottles, and an old banjo. Kenny idly picks it up and strums the first few bars of the Duelling Banjos theme...

Meanwhile the water is choppy and seems to be flowing faster, through a ravine with near-vertical walls. Someone should eventually guess that they may be heading for rapids or a waterfall. Don't worry, they'll run into other problems first...

As the boat passes a rock shelf on the left bank of the river, some "logs" that are lying there surge into action and are revealed to be large alligators. There are two alligators, or one per player character for larger groups of characters:

Alligators *Attack:* Bite (6) *Success:* 6 *Armour:* -2 all attacks *Hits:* 8 *Notes:* Strength (4)

❀If nothing is done and everyone stays well away from the sides of the boat the alligators start to bite at it, their teeth quickly tearing holes in the tough plastic; fortunately it will take a while to deflate. Before this happens the alligators break off the attack, and swim away as the boat hits the rapids. Everyone aboard is "attacked" 1-3 times by the rocks (2 dice attack, success 6—nobody should lose more than half their hits) as the boat spins and eventually sinks, washing up on another

rocky shelf at the base of another steep cliff. There are more alligators in the water below the rapids, and they soon begin to eye the adventurers hungrily... Time to climb.

✻Red Ken (or someone else with similar Animal Handling talents or an appropriate Mystic Power) can try to talk to the alligators. Unfortunately they're mostly interested in food, and the adventurers don't have anything they'd want to eat. But if Ken is persuasive enough (this should be acted out, with the alligators hissing replies as he talks—naturally only Ken understands them) they will push the boat to a rocky shelf as above. They stay nearby in the water, watching the adventurers hungrily, and Ken should soon guess that his charm may eventually be overcome by their hunger... Time to climb.

✻If the adventurers start to fight the alligators they will have to expose themselves to direct attacks; the alligators can leap up to bite a sword arm or hand as a weapon is used. However, if someone manages to dig a knife or sword into an alligator it swims away bleeding, dragging the boat behind it towards a rocky shelf as above. More alligators pursue the boat, maddened by the smell of blood, making it clear that it isn't safe to linger... Time to climb.

Climbing the cliff (about 70 ft. high) isn't actually very difficult; there are plenty of hand- holds and small ledges, and even Kenny and Ness will be able to manage it without too much trouble if given an occasional helping hand. Kenny brings the banjo if nobody else does. The person taking the lead should make an east Athlete roll twice, the next person needs to roll once, everyone else uses the safe route that the first two have found.

At the top of the cliff, as far as the eye can see, is endless desert, punctuated by a few giant cacti. Fergie's eagle eye will reveal some faint lizard tracks, and an undulating ripple in the sand which may have been left by a large snake more recently. It's faint, but on an easy Thinking roll (+2 dice for this skill) she'll trace it twenty or thirty yards, to a crack in the rock. Anyone else will need at least two successes. The crack conceals two adult rattlesnakes and eleven of their young, with another three eggs on the verge of hatching. Anyone putting a hand in will be bitten immediately.

Rattlesnake *Attack:* Bite (2)/Venom (5) dice *Success:* 6/5+ *Hits:* 3 *Notes:* Speed (2)

Ken can talk to them if present; they don't have much to say, but if asked nicely one will come out and point the adventurers towards the nearest "two legs", a "wet place" in the direction of "the rising sun", East away from the river. It takes "lots of days" to get there, but of course that's from a snake's perspective. Needless to say Ken shouldn't let anyone kill it.

Without Ken all that the adventurers can really do is wait for a snake to emerge at dusk (several hours later) and kill and eat it, hopefully without being bitten. Assume that they remember to cut off the head and venom sacs! Without help from the snakes there is nothing obvious to indicate the right direction, and it's likely that they will decide to stay near the river, possibly following the bank in hopes of finding some sign of civilisation. In this case after an hour or so they should find their first trace of human life; a small cairn of stones topped with a horse's skull, its nostrils pointing a little North of East (if they went South) or a little South of East (if they went North). If the cairn is excavated (an exhausting job in the heat) they'll eventually find some beef bones and flattened baked bean cans. If the canyon wall is checked there are easy hand-holds all the way down to the river, where a rock ledge (similar to the one where the raft was wrecked but larger) makes a good landing place. Some of the hand-holds have been improved with chisels. Unfortunately there are no boats below, just a couple of alligators sunning themselves. If anyone casts around for more clues they'll find another can in the sand, twenty yards inland from the cairn in

the direction the skull's nostrils were pointing. Atop a distant rise in that direction is the faint silhouette of another cairn, the first of a trail leading inland.

During the desert trek Ness occasionally prays to the action figure of Homer he carries in his pocket; in fact he is using the radio concealed inside it to try to contact his mercenaries, but they aren't responding. He's careful to say nothing to arouse anyone's suspicions.

After walking for two hours or so the party tops a sand dune and see the unmistakable shape of a palm tree, shimmering in the distance above the dunes. As they get closer more trees are visible—and after another couple of dunes the adventurers start to hear a faint noise, which they gradually realise is music. Closer still, and they recognise drums and the twang of a sitar. If nobody else says anything, Ness looks grave and whispers "Indians..."

Indians...

There are about fifty Indians, including women and children, camped around a large oasis. They have several large tents, a fire pit (with a spit on which an emu is being roasted), and some horses and steam wagons with broad wheels for sand. They wear traditional Sikh dress, and the men (thirty in all) are armed with daggers, swords, and bows or rifles. They wear war paint and have feathers in their turbans, and the different patterns of paint and feathers show that they come from several tribes. Their leaders are recognisable by the number of feathers in their turbans, and have better weapons:

25 Indian Braves *Attack:* Martial Arts (4), Marksmanship (3)
Success: 6 *Hits:* 2 *Notes:* Athlete (2), Speed (1), dagger, sword +1, rifle +1 or long bow +1.
5 Indian Chiefs *Attack:* Martial Arts (4), Marksmanship (3)
Success: 5+ *Hits:* 5 *Notes:* Athlete (2), Strength (2), Speed (1), dagger, sword +1, rifle +2 or long bow +2

As the men talk heatedly four sari-clad girls perform a decorous dance, accompanied by others playing drums and sitars.

Given the odds, and Diana's dislike of unprovoked combat, it's probable that the adventurers will try to find out what the Indians are doing before leaping into action. From a distance they appear to be conducting some sort of council of war. In fact they are having a barbecue before heading down to the river for the annual inter-tribal river surfing competition and alligator hunt. They aren't planning any violence, but at the moment tempers are slightly high because nobody has remembered to arrange for an impartial umpire. Their surfboards are currently aboard the steam wagons.

Any scout going close must make a Luck roll and a Thief roll to avoid detection. In play-tests Fergie often volunteered to take a closer look, and of course she is remarkably unlucky. She invariably stumbled into more Indians who raised the alarm. This usually ended with her captured, and the rest of the group making some sort of move to rescue her.

It's impossible to anticipate every possible action of players; they might walk in and request the Indians' help, decide on an entirely unprovoked attack, attempt to steal some horses or a truck and escape unnoticed, or do something else entirely. If someone is captured the Indians will be expecting trouble, which doesn't help:

❀Walking in and asking for help is a gamble. Everyone should know that Indians resent all pale-faces, with good reason. King Martin Luther's missionaries have been trying to convert them to his religion at gunpoint, Uncle Sam's empire is expanding into their territories, and Emperor Norton's empire was largely built on land their ancestors owned, although he has been trying to arrange to compensate them. Even foreigners such as Diana and Fergie will be resented at first glance, but Diana's reputation is known everywhere, and if she proves who she is they will probably be reasonably cooperative. Once they are convinced they will get old magazines containing her photograph and ask for her autograph. Unfortunately, this may cause a problem. The Indians will tolerate Americans such as Gates or Hubble if Diana vouches for them. However, if they know who Kenny is they will see a chance to use him as a hostage to get their lands back from Norton, and a good deal more persuasion will be needed to resolve the situation. And there are often photographs of Kenny in the magazines that give Diana so much attention. Fortunately Diana can be very persuasive. This ought to end with the Indians agreeing to loan Diana a steam wagon and maps for the long trek to Boston or back to Dallas—they have no cellphones or radios, so no way to arrange a speedy rescue—while Kenny negotiates some compensation payments with the chiefs. Before setting off the group are entertained by the Indians (who will want Diana to judge the surfing competition later) inside one of the tents, which looks strangely like the interior of the Taj Mahal, as the next scene begins...

✺Stealing a truck or horses won't be easy; there are a lot of Indians around, and they are a proud warrior race who hate thieves. Getting close needs rolls as above, stealing anything requires a minor miracle. The most likely result is that the adventurers, Kenny, and Ness will be escaping across the desert, pursued by an enraged war-band, with very little idea which way to go, as the next scene begins...

✺An unprovoked attack is hardly Diana's style, but if the players insist... The Indians won't go down quietly, and most are armed. Women and cute children are cut down in the cross-fire, and as the fight continues Diana experiences a strange tingling sensation, a sudden feeling that she is somehow less of a star than she was. When she looks in a mirror she will see that her hair is less tidy, and there are some bloodstains on her leathers. Take off 5 Status from Diana and 3 from everyone else, and any hits resulting from this change in Status. If the fight continues until the Indians are wiped out her Status drops by 10 and her sword shatters. At the end the adventurers have food and transport but no maps or real idea of their location. Moreover, they should find that one of the women was talking into a cell-phone (which has been shot and is now useless) before she died. By the time they reach the outside world news of the massacre will be everywhere, and Diana's reputation will be badly tarnished. But there will be another important scene first...

Before I Kill You...

Ness has been attempting to summon his mercenaries; they arrive in a huge steam-powered armoured personnel carrier, carrying Dallas Sanitation Department insignia, with a turret fitted with a rotary cannon. There are fifteen mercenaries led by three sergeants, plus a driver.

15 Mercenaries *Attack:* Martial Arts (4), Marksmanship (6) *Success:* 6 *Hits:* 3 *Notes:* Athlete (2), Speed (2), Strength (1), Machine gun +1, Nunchuks, grenades x4.

3 Sergeants *Attack:* Martial Arts (6), Marksmanship (8) *Success:* 5+ *Hits:* 4 *Notes:* Athlete (2), Strength (2), Speed (2), Machine gun +2, Katana +2, grenades x 4

Driver *Attack:* Martial Arts (4), Marksmanship (6) *Success:* 6 *Hits:* 3 *Notes:* Driver (3), Speed (2), Pistol.

APC *Speed:* 50 *Armour:* -3 *Hits:* 15 *Notes:* Machine Gun +2

The transparent gun turret (armour -1) is apparently occupied by Frank Nitti; in fact this is Landmines in disguise, but he's quite at home operating the machine gun, and will shortly do so.

Before any fighting begins Ness pulls his gun and grabbs Kenny, taking him hostage and telling Diana and friends to surrender; "If you're really cooperative I might let you live..." Given half a chance he'll explain his (revised) master plan, to kill Kenny and blame it on the bungling adventurers and the Indians. With Kenny out of the way it ought to be a couple of years before anyone starts the negotiations again.

The adventurers should be able to deal with Ness very quickly; meanwhile the Indians will start to fight the mercenaries, and it's likely that the adventurers will quickly join in.

When the chaos is at its height "Nitti" starts firing the APC's machine gun, indiscriminately killing the Indians and mercenaries. If Ness is still on his feet he'll try to take command; the next burst from the machine gun slices him in two. Oddly the gunner doesn't shoot the adventurers or Kenny; Landmines wants to gloat a little first.

It's probable that the adventurers will knock out the APC fairly quickly; Landmines then assumes his true form (a transformation which takes a round, during which he can do nothing else) with a mini-gun replacing his hand and begins to "play" with them, shooting or punching to wound rather than to kill, while taking out the remaining mercenaries and Indians.

This usually boils down to simultaneous attacks by several characters, taking advantage of the cover offered by the APC and the distracting presence of the Indians and mercenaries to whittle down Landmines' hit points. This need not necessarily be settled entirely by combat; for example, in one play-test Gates tried to use his laptop computer to hack Landmines' cyborg electronics; it worked for a few seconds, giving Diana a chance to hit him, but Landmines soon used his Mystic Power as a defence which fried the laptop. Later Fergie took control of the APC and rammed him, this was treated as an attack using Driving plus Martial Arts.

If Landmines is eventually killed he falls apart, and his head rolls towards Diana's feet. Abruptly the eyes pop open and the head says "Well done! Your capacity for violence continues to grow. Soon you will be truly fit to become my bride. Now we shall test your capacity for survival." The eyes close, and the head starts to tick loudly. It explodes as a grenade two rounds later, the rest of his body quietly vanishes.

If Landmines isn't killed (it's unlikely but possible) he'll carry on slaughtering the Indians and mercenaries until only Diana and her friends survive, kill the horses and destroy all other forms of transport, then laugh contemptuously and vanish, leaving the adventurers stranded in the desert.

The most likely result is the death of most of the mercenaries, some of the Indians, and Ness, and the temporary death of Landmines. Most of the adventurers and many of the Indians are wounded, and the camp and their vehicles are wrecked. If the adventurers have done well some of the mercenaries will be taken alive and will eventually be able to testify that Ness hired them.

It takes a day or two to look after the wounded; Diana and friends might possibly be able to leave earlier in the APC, but without a native guide it's going to be a long haul to Boston. Meanwhile one of the medicine men offers to exorcise the cellphones, if any have survived; it's a long ceremony, but eventually it ought to be possible to call Norton and request help. Alternatively, anyone with Science can try to dry them, but it's a difficult task. Once the call is made a rescue helicopter arrives a couple of hours later, carrying medical supplies and doctors. It'll fly Diana and friends out to Boston.

Into The Sunset...

At Boston airport (a grass strip with a few biplanes parked in the middle distance) Diana and co. are met by Norton. With Ness out of the way and the mercenaries testifying to his crimes, Kenny (or his successor if Kenny was killed) will have no trouble making an agreement with the next leader of the Untouchables, a carefully timed end to their segregation which will make the last of them free (and able to vote for him) just before the next election.

Diana's bike and any other vehicles or horses are waiting at the airport. As she and her friends check them out her cellphone (or a replacement provided by Norton) rings, and she listens intently as a panicked voice at the other end tells her about another crisis. She turns to her friends and says "Come on, we've work to do..." as the music starts to play and the credits rise up the screen....

Give players 5 bonus points apiece if they survived the adventure, Kenny wasn't killed, and the body count was relatively low. Additionally, points should be added or subtracted as follows:

Group Bonuses & Penalties

-3   The adventurers massacred the Indians.
-2   Kenny was killed.
-2   Ness was killed but his plot wasn't uncovered.
+2   The Indians were contacted peacefully

Individual Bonuses & Penalties

+2   Blocking a bullet meant for Kenny.
+2   Defusing the bomb.
+1   Per unnecessarily complicated but in-genre stunt.
+1   Per in-genre remark etc.
+2   For making the referee laugh
-2   Killing anyone who doesn't deserve it.

Disclaimer: No Indians, Untouchables, or Alligators were harmed in the making of this episode, but as usual Landmines, God of War, took a battering. Kids, Landmines comes back from the dead, you don't, so please don't try these stunts at home!

Appendix: Virtual Campaigns

As a variant on the "alternate world" suggested for this game it's possible to run campaigns set thousands of years in the future in which the characters are "sensie" actors, equipped with a variety of disguised high-tech gadgets to give them their amazing powers, and hypnotised to ensure that they act and think like the characters they are portraying. Players can be aware of this, or may initially believe that their characters genuinely live in the "Diana..." world, as you prefer. This change makes no real difference to play (the same rules are used, and powers have the same effects), but the referee has the option to set adventurers in the "real" world, when the characters are in their "actor" identities, lack many of the powers and abilities described above, but have access to whatever technology seems appropriate to the era. Suitable technology includes routine interplanetary or interstellar flight, antigravity, and very powerful AIs.

This change is especially appropriate if you want to use this setting with another game system, especially one that emphasises realism such as GURPS. Run the "Diana" world with simplified cinematic rules, the "real" world with gritty realism.

About Sensies

Sensies have been around for centuries, and are still the most popular form of non-interactive entertainment; first person virtual reality which includes the thoughts of the viewpoint character, recorded via a grid of implanted electrodes and transmitters. The highest forms of the art can extend to multiple layers of conscious and subconscious thought and association; even the level used for most entertainment routinely includes surface thoughts and emotions. A few (extremely highly paid) actors and actresses can control their own minds to this level of performance; most require hypnosis. In a fantasy series like Diana... the hypnosis is also used to stop the viewpoint (player) characters noticing the equipment and techniques which are used to help them perform their feats of strength, dexterity, and magic. Because this is a lengthy process, the actors spend days at a time in character, with the production company recording all events and all viewpoints then editing a coherent(?) narrative from the terabytes of data received. It isn't possible to program them with anything as rigid as a script; NPCs (the supporting cast) provide the actors with motivation, the rest is unconscious improvisation.

Non-viewpoint characters (e.g. NPCs) are usually non-hypnotised actors, but may also be expendable remote-controlled androids (usually built to "die" messily as required), holograms, or whatever else meets the needs of the plot.

Props are almost always "smart", remote controlled and incorporating tiny computers, to ensure that they will perform as the plot requires; for example, Diana's arrows are guided by seeker heads and can twist and swerve through the air to hit a target even if something else is in the way. This is normally done as inconspicuously as possible, but trick shots, with arrows, bullets, and other projectiles ricocheting off rocks and walls to hit otherwise-impossible targets, are a regular feature of the show. Weapons are also built to minimise wounds while appearing to do a lot of damage; most are made of nanobot-based polymorphic pseudo-metal which can change its shape. If an arrow hits a human target it releases a spray of fake blood, the tip steers to avoid bones and major blood vessels, and the barbs retract, making it easy to pull them out of a wound. The barbs extrude again as the arrow emerges. All of these functions can be over-ridden by the production company.

The cast are all injected with medical nanobots before recording begins. These provide total immunity from disease and can heal any wound short of death in a matter of minutes. They can also be used to simulate any disease (including wound infections and poisoning) as needed, under remote control. It isn't pleasant for the person affected, but that's how actors earn the big bucks. Note that medical nanobots are tailored to the body chemistry of their carrier, and can't be spread by blood droplets or transfusions; in any other body they will self-destruct to avoid triggering immunological problems. Nanobots are expensive, and broken down by the body after two to three weeks, another reason to record continuous sessions whenever possible.

If it is necessary for a viewpoint character to die (for example as part of a dream sequence, or because the actor wants to leave the series) the action continues until the victim is unconscious or in shock, then a "freeze" signal is sent to everyone's implants and a medical team moves in to replace the injured character with an identically injured android, and cure the actor's wounds. If all else fails a clone can be grown and given the actor's memories, which are backed up before each recording session—expensive, and yet another reason to record continuous sessions whenever possible. Naturally none of the characters remember that any time has passed when recording is resumed, although they may have spent hours or days doing other things. Similar techniques are used if it is necessary for an object or person to appear or disappear, or if the nanobots fail and more intensive medical care is needed.

Variants

Who Are These Guys...?
(suggested by Michael Cule)

In a dimension hopping game, the adventurers might accidentally arrive in a new world, without realising that they are on the vast Diana... set. At first it simply seems to be a rather strange world, but gradually the players should notice oddities. The producers don't interfere ("Who are these guys? They're great! Which of the scriptwriters came up with them?" "None of them, VC. We're a bit worried about the direction the plot's taking...." "Worried? Have you seen these ratings?" "Maybe we could make a spin-off series...") and soon start to throw in plot twists expressly designed to keep the adventurers busy and confused. Note that some aspects of the environment, such as magical healing, will not work for outsiders except as noted above!

Gladiators

The set is a penal colony. The "actors" are condemned prisoners, programmed to act out these violent fantasies on each other instead of society. Think of it as a prime-time gladiatorial arena. In this case magical healing won't work, and death is real and final. Everyone on the set (with the exception of a few androids) genuinely believes that they are in the "Diana..." world. If one of the main viewpoint characters is killed everyone is "frozen" (see below) while another prisoner, surgically altered to match the victim, is put in their place. If this option is used the adventurers will initially be unaware of the truth, but should gradually spot small betraying details that lead to the ultimate revelation and a chance of escape.